DANCING ON A
SILVER MOON

AN ALEXANDRA THE GRATE NOVEL

MARGIE ZATS

WISE
CREATIVE ★ PUBLISHING
Ink

Print ISBN: 978-1-63489-947-5

eBook ISBN: 978-1-63489-948-2

Dedicated to every woman who
choreographs her dreams

1

NEW DOORS OPEN

I t was a pounding that shook the earth. Perhaps if she could have run fast enough, far enough, to hide in the contours of a billowing cloud, Alexandra could have been spared. But that was not possible. A single hammer determined what was to be.

"There we have it, Ms. Silvers. The sign is in for all to see."

The realtor's assistant stood back, proudly admiring the bright red "Sold" sign he had secured in the ground. The ground of the lawn in front of the house—excuse me, the home—where Alexandra had lived for what she felt was forever.

"Got a nice place here," he mused. "The new family should like it. Well, I'd better get back to the office. Good luck with your condo."

With that, the young man picked up his tools, packed the unused new-listing pamphlets into a briefcase, and offered his hand to the woman who stood silently beside him.

Alex had not heard a word of what he'd said. Too consumed by thought, she numbly returned his handshake. This boy, this novice in life, could not grasp what that square of plywood represented. She labored for something pleasant to say. Anything. But the words wouldn't come.

Stop it, Alex, she reprimanded herself. He had not made today happen; he was only doing his job. Nevertheless, he was the bearer of all sadness. It was his hands that had bruised her heart with the hammer.

Her "Goodbye and thank you" would have to suffice. Alex turned away from him toward the winding cement walkway leading to the front entrance. She heard a car door close and the hum of an ignition behind her. Good—he was gone. She was alone. Instinctively Alex went into her kitchen, her companion for so many years. She sank into the closest chair and surveyed the room as if she had never seen it before.

What would the new occupants change? Which exquisite details would they dare to tamper with? Would they respect any of this history? Could they possibly understand that the small corner cabinet needed to squeak hello upon opening? That the clay pots there on the ledge above the sink had been granted permission long ago to stain small circles into the wood grain? The fresh dill and chives they provided had pleased so many guests over the years.

What memories would be ravaged in the name of "updating," of being more contemporary? The new intruders in this gallery would not, could not comprehend what hallowed hardwood she stood upon. Each creak in the floorboard and handle that needed tightening carried a story. Cherished friends, invading the room even before dinner was served, had extolled the platters brimming over with gravied beef and buttered pasta. The sweet sound of their laughter infused the walls.

Now the only noise to be heard was a sigh so deep it could have emerged from the very floor in question. But it was enough to startle her back to the present. Like a robot, Alex stood up, took a look at her watch, and, as if to discipline herself, announced, "It's time to get busy."

Shaken from her nostalgic dream, she straightened to her full height and forced herself toward the doorway. Out of the kitchen, out of the years that were good—but gone.

Maybe I'll call David. This is an easy time to catch him. Alex searched for her purse but for no logical reason. It was there, as always, waiting on the hall table. *Where,* she thought, *will I find such a niche in a condo without a foyer?* She grabbed the purse, fumbled inside it for the cellphone, and called her son's number. After two rings a pleasant baritone voice responded.

"Hi, Mom! How're you doing with the big move?"

"Oh, David, the 'Sold' sign went up today. It was hard to look at the reality, you know."

"I know, Mom, but you're doing the right thing. The house is too big for you. You're better off with someplace compact. Someplace easy and safe."

"You're right. But think of all I have to leave behind."

"C'mon, Mom. You were beginning to use those walls as a fortress. Your hiding place, far from the world surrounding you. I saw it, even if you didn't. You're not leaving anything worthwhile behind. You're taking all that matters."

"But, David ..."

"Memories, Mom, all those memories. All that love can never be left behind. That's all you need."

Alex couldn't believe what she was hearing. Where could all this wisdom be coming from? Surely not the young man who thought life was a never-ending party at which he was an honored guest.

Alex held the phone close to her cheek, as if by doing so she could touch her son.

"Thank you, David. Thanks for being smarter than me. I love you."

"Love you too, Mom. Just relax. Everything will be fine—and, oh, don't look at that damn sign."

Alex couldn't help laughing as she heard David's goodbye.

She plunged the phone back into her purse, turned into the lengthy hall, and ascended the stairway.

Which room should she first pillage? Which closet to excavate? She had already delivered mounds of household items to a nearby charity. What remained were all her favorites: keepsakes to be handed to David and whomever shared his future. It was all too overwhelming. The computer waited on the desk. Alex looked online for professional packers, selected her best option, and told the receptionist to send a crew over as soon as possible. Whatever it cost, it would be worth it. Then she went into her bedroom and, without kicking off her shoes, stretched out on the bed and put her feet up on the white linen bedspread. She'd had it for today. She plumped the pillows behind her shoulders, but as she did so the sign in the yard below came into view in the large bay window.

Oh, my God! I can't escape that thing! Alex turned away, grabbed a magazine from her nightstand, and opened it wide to cover her face. The words that followed would have made a longshoreman blush. Unexpectedly she smiled, realizing that *sold* is also a four-letter word.

The next morning, way too early for a second cup of coffee, a large van pulled into the driveway. A throng of red-uniformed helpers poured out like clowns from a circus car, to pack and carry Alexandra Silvers to her new destination. Busy bees bearing boxes and tape swarmed into the rooms, leaving them barren according to her instructions.

Up the elevator, down the corridor, second door on the right—this condo was the final destination. The manager had left the keys dangling from a ribbon on the door handle and a note wishing her welcome and happy times ahead.

Alex hesitated for a moment. If only David could have been standing there with her. If only anyone could have been beside her! Her thoughts flew back to many years before, when she and Steven had entered their house together; the same house that now belonged to a new family. Steven, husband of so long ago. Did he even know—or care—that she had moved? Had David told his father? Being a pragmatist (as lawyers are) Steve probably muttered that it was "a good idea at her age" and then continued on with his own priorities.

Alex shrugged off the memory of her former husband. She turned the key and opened the doorway of hope.

The condo faced west so the afternoon sun flooded the room with beams of light.

Alex had tried working with a decorator but found she could only express herself in food terms. The woman couldn't grasp the concepts, so Alex decided to decorate the place herself. It became a buffet of colors, vibrant and unique. Most of the old furniture was out of scale, too bulky for the smaller square footage, so a new buttercream leather sectional was selected for her living room. The textured walls were painted in butterscotch with golden maize accents. Sophisticated, yet cozy. A place anyone would call home, if only for a visit.

The kitchen, however, was designed for people who eat out. No corner for a freezer to stockpile the trays of fudge brownies and cherry cheesecakes a conscientious chef keeps on hand. No counter space for all the necessary appliances. Alex would have to compensate. It would be a challenge, but the extra linen closet could become a pantry. Guests might be surprised to find pie pans in their bathroom vanity, but it would work. Except for tonight.

Thoughtful friends had sent a basket of cheese and crackers and a bottle of white wine. Alex opened everything, sat down on her yet-unpaid-for couch and ate until the wine took effect. She thought about staying just where she was. Content. Tucked neatly into a corner, quite like an apple in a dumpling. She struggled with the temptation, but propriety forced her up and down the hallway to her bedroom.

The bed was yet unmade. No matter. Alex clutched the

quilt, threw it around herself, and sprawled down onto the bare mattress. Nine hours later she woke up refreshed.

The new bedroom had only two windows, but they were large and allowed a burst of morning to brighten the entire space. Alex stood up, stretched vigorously to relieve the stiffness of sleep, and looked around at the encompassing mess.

It would take her the rest of her life to sort all this out. Indeed, it did look that way. Boxes, some labeled and some not, had seemingly reproduced themselves during the night. They obstructed Alex's path. Careful not to trip, she maneuvered to the bathroom, which remained without towels or a soft rug to protect her toes from the cold tile floor. She flipped on the lights ... and jumped backwards. A massive mirror, quite the length of the cabinets, glared mercilessly at a woman who had slept in her clothes the night before. A row of lights shined brilliantly, unaware of the grimace that reflected back. "My God, I look like an unmade bed!"

It made her laugh. It also made her find her favorite lavender shower lotion to put the formerly pristine Alexandra together again.

The coffee pot, which she located, surprisingly, in a box marked *kitchen,* supplied the caffeine necessary to begin the herculean task of assembling one room after another into livable shape. Within weeks the empty condo transformed into the attractive model on the advertising brochure.

While rooms can be improved, walls cannot be extended by wishing them so. On her first morning, Alex reached into the refrigerator for a couple of eggs, cracked them into a bowl, and with barely a ballerina's pirouette, threw the shells into the sink's disposal. "Hmmm—a chef's hole in one!" she exclaimed, pleased to be mastering her culinary claustrophobia.

Before she could even eat breakfast her handbag began ringing. Alex spun around, instinctively seeking the hall table where it had resided for years. However, there was no longer a table. There was no longer a hall, only a short passageway leading one room into the other.

"Where did I put that thing?" She followed the sound into her bedroom where, among a pile of clothes heaped on a chair, she found her cell.

"Hey, Mom, are you there? I couldn't image you'd get lost in that cubicle!"

"Yes, David, I'm here, dear," They both paused to laugh at the absurdity.

"Just called to see how you're doing. I'm really sorry I'm here and you're on your own there."

"Darling, don't apologize. It's more important you stay at school to finish your master's. How are you doing with those classes?"

"Tough, Mom, really tough. I can't wait to graduate."

"My son, the tax accountant! Never dreamed you'd choose that career. I always thought you'd go into something more creative."

"Well, helping people stay out of jail is an art form."

Again they both laughed.

"Okay, gotta go study. Good luck in the new pad. I'll help you when I get home."

"By that time everything will be done, David."

"That's the idea." To her delight her son, the sun of her life, nearly giggled just as he'd done as a child. The phone turned off but Alex held it for an extra moment, not wanting to let go of the most important person in her world.

Within minutes the phone rang again. This time Alex answered quickly. A young woman's voice began, "Hello, may I please speak with Alexandra?"

"With whom am I speaking?"

"I'm Amelia from Northridge College. Dean Benneton's assistant. He asked me to remind you about the faculty reception on Thursday. May I tell him to plan on you?"

Embarrassed, Alex stammered, "Yes, certainly. I received your invitation, but you see, I just now moved and I must have misplaced it and forgotten to respond. Please tell the dean I'll be delighted to attend."

"Thank you, I will." Amelia spoke in her most professional tone, but Alex could tell she was new to the job.

Settling her household was suddenly demoted to a lesser priority. It had been winter, more than half a year ago, when Alex first met the dean—quite by accident.

Years before Alex had been signed to do a cooking show, *Alexandra the Grate*, featuring foods on the grill. It was created to promote products sold at the Culinary Arts Center where she taught classes. It hadn't been her idea or really her career goal, and she hadn't truly enjoyed the exhilaration of performing. But it pleased Ted Hudson, the CEO—and a very special friend in her life at the time—so she had agreed to an extensive contract. Maybe it was the fear of change, or perhaps destiny, but Alex had convinced herself the money was too good to stop.

So, that night months before, she was rehearsing in the studio as usual, standing with a spatula in hand in front of a pan of hashed brown potatoes, hoping to entice a hungry viewing audience. Without warning, the door burst open and a middle-aged gentleman appeared beside her. She was too startled to even exclaim the obvious "What are you doing here?" The intruder stared back, just as amazed to discover himself on-set and the target of the director's bellow, "For God's sake man, how did you get in here?" The cameramen began to chuckle, and needless to say, the rehearsal came to an immediate end.

Quite flustered, the stranger stammered something about directions to a nearby studio where he was to be interviewed. Red-faced, he apologized profusely for imposing as a production assistant gently took him by the arm and escorted him to his proper destination.

It had seemed like a sketch on late-night comedy. After a few minutes to regain composure, Alex and the crew continued on. It was getting late, and she felt tired.

As usual, the day had been long. When they wrapped, Alex could only think about getting home to relax before the next day's shooting. The parking lot was well lit and her car just steps away. But the crackling of footsteps behind her on the snowy path made her walk quickly, anxious to get within range of clicking open the door.

"Please let me apologize." A man's voice pleaded from behind her.

"What did you say? I couldn't hear you well." Alex deliberately asked him to repeat himself hoping to detect his motive. Was he a menace or simply a persistent voice in the night?

He continued, "I just wanted to say I was sorry for intruding, for interrupting your concentration."

It was a gentle voice with good diction. Alex turned to see a stocky, gray-haired man approach. It was the person who had interrupted her rehearsal earlier. His eyes were friendly and his hands spread open in an apologetic gesture as he caught up to her.

Alex couldn't help smiling. This kindly man was so sincere and obviously still embarrassed.

"Of course you're forgiven," she said. "Accidents like this happen. Maybe it was the aroma of all those potatoes that lured you."

They stood there together, and the chill of the night air was warmed by the clasp of hands.

"Let me introduce myself. I'm James Benneton—and you are?"

"Alexandra Silvers, resident culinary instructor. May I ask your profession?"

"I'm in education too. Perhaps you've heard of Northridge Community College? It's not far from here. I'm the dean of continuing education. That's the reason I was here at the station tonight. I was interviewed about job opportunities."

"Oh, how interesting." Alex opened her mouth to continue but a gust of wind swept past her face. For a moment she was unable to speak as a shiver overwhelmed her.

"Ms. Silvers, you've given me an idea, but it's much too cold to discuss it tonight. May I contact you at a better time?"

"Of course, Mr. Benneton." With nearly numb fingers Alex managed to open her purse and extract a business card from her wallet. "Let's talk when we're more comfortable," she added, hoping to conclude the conversation. James Benneton nodded politely, turned, and disappeared into the night, allowing Alex to reach her car and turn the heat on full blast.

The weeks passed, and with so much to do Alex hadn't given a thought to the man in the parking lot. That is, not until the phone awakened her just after nine on a Thursday morning. Ordinarily she would have been up and better prepared for the call, but the previous day she'd caught a nasty head cold and the antihistamine had done its job.

The caller asked if this was the Silvers residence. "Yes, it is," Alex hoarsely replied.

"Hello, Ms. Silvers. It's Amelia from Dean Benneton's office. Northridge College, remember? He's spoken with you before."

"Of course, Amelia. A cold has gotten the best of me, and I'm rather slow this morning. What can I do for you?"

"The dean would like to meet with you whenever you have time. Could you check your calendar, please?"

"The dean wants to meet with me? I can't imagine why." But as much as she prodded, Alex couldn't get information from the guarded assistant.

"He asked me to phone you and set up an appointment," she replied.

Alex reached for the datebook on her desk. "Well, tell Dean

Benneton I have next Tuesday afternoon open. By then I should be feeling better, too."

"How is two p.m. in his office on campus?"

Alex agreed quickly, if only to conclude the call so she could find a much-needed tissue. "Fine, Amelia, I'll be there if I survive. Please tell the dean I said thank you."

"I will, and I hope you feel better. Drink some orange juice." Amelia hung up without waiting for Alex to agree.

The week vanished along with the congestion. Alex had conflicting feelings about her meeting with the dean. Flattered but curious, she wondered what he could possibly want to discuss. Amelia had been so vague, as though her job depended on a mysterious secret.

Alex arrived at the dean's office a little early. Worried that she'd have trouble locating the right building she had allowed an extra ten minutes. Now, not wanting to look overanxious, she remained in the car and watched all the energetic students, boasting the summer of youth, scurrying along to their next class. How could it have been so long since she, too, raced up the stairs, eager to learn and free to capture the elusive future?

Her watch gave her permission; at last it was time. Inside the building, a small plaque displaying the dean's name was evident on the first door. She tapped on the door and was directed to enter a room that was much too small for all the furniture crowded into it. Oak cabinets jammed with books and a couple of metal files huddled together like old companions. One without the other would not do.

"Hello, you must be Ms. Silvers. I'm Amelia," a voice called out from behind a cluttered desktop.

Amelia was obviously the most recent addition to the office —younger than the furniture. Her eyes looked strained and her hair was pulled back in a no-nonsense fashion. It was apparent she was intent on the business of the day.

"The dean is expecting you. I'll let him know." She picked up the phone and announced that his two o'clock had arrived.

Within seconds an office door opened and Dean James Benneton, PhD, head of the School of Continuing Education, stood before Alex. A smile stretched over the entire width of his face as he said hello.

"Amelia, hold my calls. Ms. Silvers and I need time." He ushered his puzzled guest into his office—or, to be more accurate, his personal library. The desk was chaotic in an organized way. Stacks of papers sat on one side while thick reference books balanced the other end. In the middle of it all, the professor settled into his chair, looking pleased to say what he had in mind.

"Ms. Silvers."

"Please, call me Alex."

"Your reputation precedes you. I've researched your website. You have a splendid résumé. After dropping into your television show and inhaling your wonderful cooking, I am pleased to offer you a teaching position here at Northridge. We're extending our culinary arts program, giving an opportunity for those students interested in earning a diploma in food service to become certified chefs. I'm confident you would be a great addition to our staff. It's my pleasure to offer you an assistant professorship."

"But ... dean, I have two jobs already. I've been teaching— although it's just Wednesday nights—at the Culinary Arts Center, and of course there is *Alexandra the Grate*. I'm very flattered, though. Thank you so much."

"Perhaps it's time to move on, Alex. This job offers security, amenities, and a retirement plan. It would give you a full position."

Alex didn't know quite what to say. But the salary was tempting and she realized she should not flatly refuse. She needed time to decide, to calculate the benefits and any liabilities. Gathering her coat around herself, as if the fabric could insulate a decision, Alex rose from her chair. "Please give me time to think this through. I'm just so surprised by your offer."

"Of course, Alex. Get back to me when you're comfortable. But I do feel it's a fine opportunity for you."

Alex shook his hand in response, walked out of the office (nodding briefly to Amelia), and managed to drive home without going through any red lights.

That evening, alone with an ample glass of pinot noir, Alex took pen to paper. The old method still worked best; one side of the sheet was pro, the other con. A list of attributes and detriments. The culinary arts class was only four sessions a month, hardly enough income to sustain herself. Besides, since Ted's departure it had never been the same. The excitement, the joy of it all had left with him. It was a time for honesty: the television show was difficult. The pressure had never lessened over the years. Maybe she would do well to stop before the audience felt she'd become boring, a has-been, too stubborn to quit before the ratings fell.

The teaching position could be stimulating, a chance to mentor young people. Besides, she had to consider retirement someday. What a comfort it would be to get a check each month.

Within a day she made the phone call.

"Yes, Dean Benneton, I will accept your offer."

Alex slept well that night. She knew she had made the right decision and vowed never to look back at what might have been.

2

SCRAMBLED EGGHEADS

G ossip travels at lightning speed, and as the students at the culinary school heard the news, Alex had much to explain. She had become a favorite after so many years, and her absence would leave an unhappy void—and a deficit in tuition renewals.

The film crew wasn't as emotional. They were conditioned to change, and after expressing regret, they began interviewing other chefs with a talent for presenting various formats. Alexandra had served her purpose. Now it would be someone else's chance to entertain an ever-expanding viewership.

James Benneton was delighted. He had taken a chance on convincing her and was quick to get a contract signed. Orientation began in late August, and school started two weeks later. A faculty party was scheduled in between.

The reception area of the Great Hall (as it was referred to with reverence) could have been used as a movie set. Windows stretched nearly the length of the room, each pane displaying famous authors and the volumes they had written. No one could actually decipher each historical figure, but collectively they made a great impression. The massive gray stone fireplace contrasted with the mahogany paneling and burgundy carpeting. Couches upholstered in antique-brown leather were surrounded by softly cushioned chairs that offered an instant welcome. Assuredly, this hall had played host to many elegant events throughout the years. And, most certainly, the walls had absorbed thousands of hushed words meant to go no further.

For once Alex did not want to be early; a half hour into the festivities seemed comfortable. When she entered, people had begun to form a line at the buffet table. The bar, already crowded, was obvious from the doorway.

"Oh, there you are, Alex. I've been watching for you." Dean Benneton's voice cut through the thunderous commotion to salvage his new appointee from an isolated entrance. "Come, let me start introducing you. So many of the faculty have heard of you. They'll be pleased you're here today."

Alex could hardly say thank you before she was guided toward a large group enjoying an animated conversation.

"May I interrupt to introduce our new associate professor, Alexandra Silvers?" the dean boomed.

A tall, rather lanky man spoke first. "Alexandra the Grate! The television chef!" Someone else chimed in, "Yes, we've watched your program. Marvelous!" Hands were extended, securing a warm welcome as everyone quipped about the show and how they, too, loved to cook. As expected, one fellow thought he was being uniquely clever by asking if they could all come to dinner some night. Alex, conditioned to that line, quickly responded, "Of course, you're all invited," though she had no intention of following through with a pot roast.

The dean escorted her around the room until Alex felt she was immersed in a cavalcade of peering faces. It was impossible to attach names to all of them. Oh well, she thought, eventually everybody will have a title.

After nearly an hour of social niceties, Alex excused herself long enough to sample some of the hors d'oeuvres on the buffet. Trying to balance the plate along with a flute of champagne—while fighting the chain on her purse, which had slipped off her shoulder—was impossible. She sank into a chair nearly out of sight, hoping no one had seen her juggling act.

"Whew," she sighed rather loudly as she settled in without spilling on herself.

"You managed that quite well," a voice from a nearby chair exclaimed. Alex turned abruptly to stare into the face of a man with a most amused smile. He'd obviously been transfixed by her contortions as she eased herself down, both hands steady on her plate while a disobedient black handbag flip flopped against her side.

"Excuse me for smiling, but I had to admire your agility. I don't think we've met. I'm Charles Coleman, with the music department."

Alex smiled and introduced herself. Charlie, as he preferred to be called, was swimming upstream in his fifties, but his demeanor contradicted every year. Graying hair too curly to be tamed fell loosely onto his forehead. The face beneath was remarkably friendly; advertisers used that look to sell products. But not for food, because Charlie obviously did not have much appetite. He was so slender, as though he'd forgotten to eat lately, that Alex the chef immediately thought of feeding him.

But his most outstanding feature was those eyes. Irrepressible, rascally—even when he was sitting quietly and talking politely, they gave him away. Deepest brown, with a suggestion of mischief not to be hidden they conveyed an undeniable message to come join him at the party. Alex could feel him looking at her as few men ever had. She could have excused herself, gotten up to leave, but she did not, for reasons she couldn't explain.

"Well, Ms. Silvers."

"Alex, please."

"Alright, Alex. When you get settled, I'll be glad to show you around."

"Thanks for the offer, Charlie, I'll remember that." But before she could continue, announcements from the other end of the room interrupted. The woman holding the microphone continued, "Now it's time for some entertainment, and there's no one more talented than our own Charlie Coleman. Let's coax him up here for a few songs on the piano. Charlie, where are you? Ah, now I see you!"

Charlie had slid down in his chair, attempting to hide. "Oh damn, they found me!"

Conversely, Alex bolted upright. "What are you talking about? What's happening?"

Acknowledging that there was no avoiding a command performance, Charlie rose to his feet and began the long trip across the room. Applause followed him to the Steinway piano (donated years before by a grateful alumni).

He had briefly explained to her his position with the music department—that he'd been on staff several years after a long career playing professionally—but Alex had no hint of just how good he was.

Within a few chords, the entire hall went silent; no one wanted to miss a note. His fingers glided effortlessly over the keys with a magician's litheness, touching their surface, then disappearing to give others a flight of fancy. Charlie played that piano with such grandeur that it seemed an instrument had been lowered from heaven so mortals could eavesdrop. For that time, every woman in the room was a little in love with Charlie Coleman—and every man wished to be him.

Finally, after enough encores, Charlie pushed the piano bench back, stood up with a nod to the crowd and walked out of view. He couldn't see, over the heads of many much taller people, if the woman he had just met remained where he'd left her. He sighed as the crowd parted and he realized that someone had taken her chair. Far across the room, near the doorway, he saw Alex saying goodnight to the dean; he had lost her for the evening. Unaccustomed to having women walk away from him, he determined he would try again. Classes were just beginning. So was Charlie.

The culinary arts building was located on the west end of the sprawling campus. Undeniably old, it was reminiscent of a structure used in a movie about an English boarding school, right down to the ivy clinging to the weathered façade. Attached by a caretaker too long ago to remember, the vines disengaged to allow only the chosen to enter through the heavy wooden doors.

Alex pushed hard against the entry, nearly dropping the carton she carried. No one offered to help, but she could feel the inquisitive stares of students encircling her.

Finally, a male voice said, "Can I help you, ma'am?" With much relief, Alex released her burden into his strong arms. "Where would you like this?" was the next question.

"Well, I'm going to the administrative suite. If I remember, it's down the hallway on the right-hand side."

The young man nodded respectfully as he realized she was new faculty. He motioned for her to follow as he led the way to a ten-by-twelve foot office around which Alexandra Silvers's life would now revolve.

The shelves were crowded with what appeared to be every cookbook ever published in America. Cartons she had previously sent had been alphabetically arranged by interns. Impressively, Alex had nearly memorized the contents of each book, so that when a reference was needed she knew exactly where to find it. It would be a great inventory for her students —including many recipes she'd personally created—and would serve as the base of her instruction.

Her office had to be efficient, for there was not a square foot to squander. Alex pulled open the shades on the only window and looked down to the parking lot; it certainly was not scenic, but at least she could see her car. It would give her security after an evening class.

Within the week the drab walls were covered with large photographs of food: platters abundant with ripe tomatoes and sweet bell peppers of yellow and green. Flaky strudels with apple slices sprinkled with cinnamon sugar and golden raisins seemed to tumble from the picture opposite. The best, however, was the photo facing the door. Framed in a gold matte finish, succulent slices of medium-rare tenderloin, oozing with au jus, nestled atop mounds of creamy mashed potatoes. Anyone entering eyed these photos with delight, along with a sudden feeling of hunger.

A desk, two chairs, and carpeting that should have been replaced years ago, made up the rest. But to Alex, this inconsequential hideaway became a haven, replacing, at least in theory, her kitchen of comfort.

The culinary classrooms on the second floor were a great contrast: large, airy, and immaculate. Adhering to a strict rule of cleanliness, there were polished stainless-steel countertops, white cabinets everywhere, and mandatory drains in the scrubbed floor. The west wall was all windows, bringing in a brightness that competed with the artificial lighting overhead. Each ingredient and every utensil could be clearly identified.

There were stations for each student: two gas burners, a small sink, a large cutting board, and an overhead rack for storage. Alex had a small desk in the far corner, but for the most part, she would be traveling between the students, inspecting and critiquing their work. A large, freestanding blackboard with the day's instructions stood near the entrance, along with a table stacked with recipes. Along the back wall were shelves of ingredients, two refrigerators, and two freezers.

The school had just refurnished, at considerable expense, the antiquated kitchen originally installed. The graduate

degree program in culinary arts had been canceled for several
years because the facilities had not met the current Health
Department standards. The newly appointed dean of continuing education had seen a potential others had not. With the
skill of a political lobbyist and a little help from the private
sector, Dr. James Benneton raised the money to reinstate the
program and attract instructors to lead the classes. And good
fortune had guided him on that cold winter's night when he
ventured into the wrong room, to find his chef du jour. He then
hired Tommy and Georgio from local restaurants to assist.

On her first day of class Alex stood by the door to greet her
students as they filed in. Already dressed in the customary
black-checked trousers and white jackets, most of them looked
eager to learn and so very young compared to her students at
the Culinary Arts Center. Those people, already established in
other professions, came for an evening of fun and good eating.
These youngsters wanted a career. *How exciting*, she thought, *to
inspire them, to make each student stretch and achieve a level of
excellence.* She smiled; it was not dissimilar to working with a
tender dough, prodded and pushed to perfection.

Everyone wore nametags and agreeably took their assigned
places. After introductions, Alex explained that although it was
customary to say "professor," here in this culinary class "chef"
was the respected title. She then reviewed the assignments of
the day, and work began. But she quickly realized a two-hour
class was not adequate for preparation, tasting, and cleanup;
she needed to simplify the meal planning. But other than that,
and the usual spills, the session ran efficiently.

Tommy and Georgio circulated through the classroom,
demonstrating techniques and giving advice. But they had been
well trained by their former executive chefs: Alex was in
charge.

A bell never sounded so welcome. The first class was over;
she had two hours before the next. Alex left soon after the

students and headed downstairs to her office, hoping that the secretary had brought lunch in from the cafeteria. She was ravenous after being surrounded by food all morning without having time to take a bite.

As she reached her desk she saw a glob of tuna on a plastic plate. Shreds of limp lettuce filled in where the salad did not. Tomorrow she'd get her own lunch.

Two bites in, the phone rang. Alex had taken too large a mouthful to speak clearly, but she answered anyway.

"Hello there, it's Charlie Coleman. Remember we met at the faculty reception? Just wanted to know how your first day is going. Alex—are you there?"

"Yes, Charlie. Excuse me. I'm just now gobbling some lunch. I dealt with food all morning. I guess it gave me an appetite."

"Well, in that case, could we have dinner some night this week? I'll take you to a nice place with big portions."

Alex was afraid she'd choke if she laughed. Swallowing quickly, she stammered for an answer. Charlie thought it was the tuna fish. In truth it was a stall.

"Oh, Charlie, thanks but I don't think so. I'm so overwhelmed with settling in. Sometime in the future perhaps."

Charlie's voice dropped to a lower octave as he said that he understood. But there was no place to go from there, and the conversation concluded with an abrupt goodbye. Alex immediately sensed she had hurt him, but she had no intention of getting involved at this time, and certainly not with Charlie Coleman!

3

SONSHINE

T he remainder of the day and the following weeks fell into place. The dreadful tuna salad was replaced with sociable meals in the staff dining room. Often Dean Benneton would stop by Alex's table just to say a few kind words or tell a little joke that wasn't really that funny. But Alex and her companions would laugh appreciatively.

After one of these corny comments a newly hired teaching assistant blurted out, "That old fellow is not too with it!"

The woman across the table gave her a reprimanding glare. "Don't be foolish! He's sharper than all of us put together. The man's brilliant, and don't you ever forget it!"

The woman rose to leave as the recipient of her scolding nearly slid under her chair.

Alex soon realized the dean's method. He knew every detail about her work: what was being accomplished and how the students were responding. His frequent chats at lunch were deliberate and purposely subtle. He could read Alex's expressions and body language to assure himself he'd made a smart choice.

Weeks dissolved into months. Charlie did not call again. Apparently one rejection was sufficient to slam a door shut. Alex did think of him on occasion, but he slipped from mind quickly. She never even ran into him on campus because the music department was on the opposite end, in a sprawling building with a view of the winding river—not the parking lot.

Her favorite gentleman caller, David, did phone his mother often, even though he was absorbed in his studies. By June he would earn his master's degree in higher finance from a prestigious East Coast university. Alex was grateful he'd be graduating without the burden of college loans. That was about all she was grateful to her former husband for. Steven Silvers, the prominent attorney-at-law, had paid his son's tuition as promised. Alex suspected it was partly out of duty and partly for bragging rights about David's impressive education. Always arrogant and looking to make an impression, Steven's love for the boy came third.

David was an only child, pampered and indulged and given his whim through life without the balance of responsibilities. Alex had been through two miscarriages before a difficult pregnancy with David. She had been ecstatic to finally hold him in her arms and this fair-haired beautiful baby learned to walk early on azure waters.

"Just wanted to call, Mom, and tell you I'll miss you this vacation. Dad invited me to Palm Springs. He's rented a house for the season. I couldn't turn down the invite. Hope it's okay. You're not mad, are you?"

"No, David, of course not, dear." As usual, she added, "Enjoy yourself. Have a great time. I'll find plenty to do here."

But when the call was over, when her falsetto dropped, Alex did her best to hold back tears of disappointment. She missed him so dearly. He was the only close family she had.

Daytime hours evaporated easily, but as the sunlit hours fell victim to encroaching winter, nighttime became more foreboding. Alone. Yes, Alex brought work home, and there was always a book by the bedside collecting dust. Sometimes she'd watch a food program on television, offering constructive criticism of the chef's presentation and proudly thinking that she could have improvised better.

But whatever she did, whatever she tried, the room ached with silence. Frequently she'd reach for a CD. Her mood that evening would make the selection. Music, the soulful searching for a sound yet to be discovered, interrupted the stillness and brought her the peace of memories—of a tenderness shared with someone so special that the feeling could never be lost to time. There she would rest and listen and watch as the radiance of a small lamp teased shadows against the darkening wall. In the morning the solitude would be blanketed with the dazzling opportunities of a new day, daring Alex to hurry and keep up.

Eight classes a week and four full days interspersed with staff meetings became routine. As demanding as her schedule was, she still felt less pressured than in previous years at the television station. How had she withstood the constant scrutiny from the director and ornery Kate, the production assistant who seemed to be physically attached to her clipboard? Perhaps it had been soldered on in her youth. Alex grinned at such an intriguing thought. She certainly didn't miss having to perform before an audience of thousands and endure the continual commentary of viewers who thought they could do as well—and be more amusing. In contrast, Alex did regret leaving the Culinary Arts Center. It had been her first job after graduating from Le Ecole de Cuisine in London so many years ago. That position had given her new direction, a sense of who she was, and the confidence to grow. She missed the people: sweet Mary, her collaborator and the friend everyone hopes to find. In her mind she saw the faces of the students, a medley of spices more flavorful than the food they prepared. Deliberately lingering, Alex hesitated before continuing to the logical—and inevitable—conclusion. Ted Hudson. He was there, smiling, just as attractive as the day they met. How she yearned for a happy ending but even in her fantasies he remained unattainable.

4

A RANGE OF TALENTS

The class curriculum was organized in levels. The students were first taught techniques. Once they had perfected using a knife—mincing and dicing and deboning—they escalated to small appliances. The art of folding in egg whites and agility with the wire whisk were next. Having conquered the fundamentals, they continued on to meal preparation. Some immediately preferred the grill station, others soups and salads, while a large group practiced pastries. A select few chose to stand at the range and sauté.

Alex, Tommy, and Georgio traded specialties as they rotated students each class. Most days the room burst with aromas of freshly baked bread and chicken simmering in sauce de vin. Even the outer hallway captured this gastronomical perfume, causing the people walking by to happily inhale.

Alex felt a new energy absorb her. After all her years of teaching, she had never sensed such gratification as she did when watching young people become inspired. The enthusiasm of this company triggered a response she'd forgotten. Maybe it brought back memories of David and his friends swarming around their kitchen, eager to watch, more eager to taste. This gathering of young lions, so poised for adventure, exhilarated her spirit. Whatever the chemistry, the classes were working and Alex felt successful.

Enter Garrett Bell. He was the student she'd been waiting for, her payback for all those years of effort. Garrett, with skin the tone of burnished copper and a brush of hair tied tightly at the nape of his neck. His deep-set eyes darted anxiously away when confronted, as if they withheld secrets never to be divulged. Here was a youth to be reckoned with; his extraordinary abilities were so evident that Alex was immediately drawn to him. Here was a student with the potential to emblazon her career with a star.

She spoke highly of him to Dean Benneton, who listened intently. It was just what he wanted to hear: a Northridge student coming forth from his School of Continuing Education, making a future illustrious reputation as an executive chef.

David, however, was not as enthusiastic. "Don't be so quick to hang a medal around his neck, Mom. He sounds too ambitious, too smart for me."

"Oh, David, don't be so skeptical. You'd like him if you knew him. He's so anxious to please."

"That's just it, Mom. Maybe too anxious!" But Alex tossed off her son's cynicism as natural resentment. Another young man was being tended in his mother's garden.

In class Alex was a professional and tried hard not to show favoritism. For the most part, everyone was given equal assignments and attention. But on occasional menus Garrett would take the lead. It was his presentation of veal Oscar with asparagus and crabmeat garnish that Alex devoured (although she was only to take a bite of competing entries). It was he who stayed after class, anxious to ask questions about the next assignment, and it was she who smiled each time she'd walk by his station. The others, if they did notice, pretended they didn't.

It was of no interest. All they cared about were the credentials on their résumés.

Winter was relenting. As snow began to melt, leaving icy patches on blackened pathways, Alex moved cautiously as she approached the stairway to her building. One step in and the cumbersome armload of books she was carrying tumbled from her arms. Instinctively she went down to retrieve them as they scattered at her feet, but her reach was short and jeopardized her balance. Within seconds Alex, too, was sprawled on the steps in a most undignified position. But she was in too much pain to be embarrassed.

Voices above her head started shouting commands. The loudest—"Take her to health service!"—could be heard above the female squeals of "Oh my God, it's Chef Silvers" interrupted by frequent "What just happened?" queries.

A campus ambulance soon drove up, and paramedics hoisted Alex onto a gurney and headed toward the infirmary, leaving a crowd of curious onlookers, all of whom would be late for class.

Alex was fortunate. Nothing was broken, which she attributed to her conscientious absorption of calcium each day. All her women acquaintances were lectured to do likewise. She had only sprained her right ankle. However, it would require wearing a clumsy blue boot for about a month. She could still walk, but driving would be a problem.

James Benneton was the first to contact her. "Alex, my dear, I wish I could chauffer you each day, but I share a car with my husband, Jack. He drops me off and then goes to his studio across town."

"Oh, Dean, that's quite all right, as long as I can still teach. Fortunately I didn't injure my mouth!"

They both managed to smile as Alex arranged the flowers he had brought her, each wishing for an easy solution to drop from the sky.

In the end it didn't fall from out of nowhere, but rather emerged from the pocket of her purse. The cell phone rang just as Alex was limping across the room to see the dean out.

"Don't rush, Alex. I'll let myself out. Goodbye now, and be well."

Before the fourth ring Alex managed to grab the phone and answer the persistent caller.

"Hi there, Chef, it's Garrett. How're you doing?"

"Well, I'm trying to adjust to being Bigfoot here. Eventually I'll manage."

"That's just it. I heard you can't drive with that bum right boot. I can pick you up. I'm going to the same place, you know."

"Oh, Garrett, thank you, but an instructor can't accept rides from a student. I really appreciate your thoughtfulness, but I must follow the rules. It's established protocol, you know."

She could sense by the silence Garrett's disappointment; he was searching for the right words. Finally: "Well, how're you gonna get to school?"

Alex smiled. The boy was actually mothering her.

"Don't worry. I've already made arrangements with a taxi service. They're even giving me a courtesy discount on my two fares a day."

"Then I guess you're all set and don't need me."

Alex knew what she should say next: "Of course I need you. You're my most talented student!"

Garrett's voice lightened, and Alex imagined the grin on his face. It was just what he was hoping to hear.

"Glad you're gettin' along."

"Thank you for thinking of me," she answered, and with that the call ended, leaving Alex holding the phone and wondering if Garrett really understood boundaries.

As long as she was home and allowed to feel sorry for herself, she decided to thump into the kitchen and bake her favorite chocolate chip cookies. She perched on a high kitchen stool for comfort. No sooner had the butter blended with the sugar than the phone rang again. Thinking how foolish she'd been to have left it in the other room, Alex debated whether to answer. But curiosity won and she managed to respond just before voicemail interceded.

"Hello, Alex. I couldn't imagine you'd be out yet. This is Charlie Coleman. I heard about your accident and wondered if I could be of any help?"

"Oh, Charlie, thanks. Yes, I certainly am home, taking it easy."

"Is there anything you need? Do you have enough groceries? But then, you probably have a good supply on hand."

"Well, as a matter of fact, I was just making myself some consolation cookies."

"What kind?"

"Chocolate chip."

There was an awkward moment. It was Alex's cue to invite him over. He waited, but the sentence he hoped for was not spoken.

"Charlie, thanks for calling, but I need to finish so I can elevate my leg. Doctor's orders."

"Okay, Alex, I'll try you another time. Maybe by then we can go dancing." Alex couldn't help but laugh. This Charlie, the piano man with the indefinable charm, also had a sense of humor. She liked that. Maybe when she felt better, he deserved an appreciative glance ... or two.

She returned to her cookie batter, baked it to a perfect golden brown, and without allowing them to cool, ate three warm gooey hunks. With a ribbon of chocolate swirling around her fingers, Alex licked them clean rather than wash her hands. Delicious! She then limped into her room, lay down on the bed, and propped a large pillow under her aching ankle.

Monday came too soon. Right on time, the taxi pulled up to the front door of Alex's building, a window rolled down, and a friendly voice shouted, "Don't move, I'm coming to get ya!" A pudgy driver jumped from the front seat and ran to assist Alex before she could say, "I'll manage myself"—which they both knew she couldn't. As much as she resisted the help, it was a relief to have a driver. It was hard just to get around lugging that mammoth blue albatross. Going upstairs to class presented a problem, but there was always the supportive arm of a student to steady her climb. It became a routine. Not that it got any easier—Alex just became used to it.

The most frustrating part of her new normal was anticipating the exact time she'd quit for the day. Last-minute phone calls or a quick chat with a student in the hallway delayed her schedule, but she was bound by her watch and the cab waiting at the curb, its meter running. Fifteen minutes from call time and Alex needed to be out the door, ready for the ride home.

All was working well until one late afternoon. Alex phoned in her request and hobbled out to the front door thirteen minutes later. It had started to sprinkle. The forecast on that early spring evening had predicted a heavy storm coming in from the western part of the state. No worry, she'd be home snug by then.

The minutes were long. It became painful standing on the hard cement sidewalk. Suddenly a cloudburst imploded, and the torrent was a fury from above. It had been too difficult to carry an umbrella along with her bag of books. She feared she might fall; her footing was jeopardized by the wet concrete beneath her. *Where is that damn cab!* she wondered. She nearly hollered it again out loud. It made her feel better. Somehow Alex managed to retrieve her phone from all the paraphernalia and called the company's number—and, of course, was put on hold. Everyone in the city must need a cab too.

As she stood there, absorbing precipitation, a car rolled up to the curb and a familiar voice called out, "Chef Silvers, come on, get in. You're getting soaked!" Alex recognized Garrett's voice. What a godsend! There was no time to question his offer; a thunderous applause sounded from the heavens.

"Here, let me help you. How long have you been standing here?"

"The taxi didn't come. Of all times that driver didn't show! Thanks, Garrett, you're a lifesaver." Alex huddled into the front seat, grateful to be spared.

"I just happened to be coming past at the right time. That's what you call luck!"

Traffic was heavy by that hour. The drone of the windshield wipers beat a dull rhythm as every light seemed to deliberately turn red on their approach. Other than giving directions, they spoke little. Alex was too uncomfortable, and Garrett needed to concentrate on his driving.

When they arrived at the condo, Alex attempted to extricate herself from the car. They could only laugh at her awkwardness.

"Here, let me help you. We don't need you falling again."

"Thanks so much. If you don't mind, I'll lean on your arm a bit. It's so hard with all this rain." They walked as fast as they could under the conditions. Entering the small vestibule, Alex grappled for her key ring, which had slid into a compartment of her purse. One look at Garrett made her exclaim, "Your jacket is soaked through! You look absolutely frozen. C'mon, I'll fix us something warm before we both get pneumonia." All Garrett could do was shiver in agreement.

The elevator was crowded. Everyone living in the building must have arrived home at the same time. Neighbors stood in silence, pressing buttons for their floor and trying to avoid being too near the dripping duo in the corner—glad for their departure on the third floor.

Keys in hand this time, Alex quickly opened the door for Garrett.

"Take off that jacket. There are towels in the guest bathroom down the hall. Grab one for me, too, please. I'll make us an herbal brew."

Alex went into the kitchen and was just filling the teakettle when she heard Garrett's footsteps behind her. "Good, you found the towels. I need one for my hair."

She extended her hand but instead felt the terrycloth cover her head like a turban. Turning around, she saw the amusement on Garrett's face.

"We must have looked like we'd been drowning at sea. I hope those neighbors of mine don't report me."

"Report you for what, getting wet?"

"For inviting you to my home."

"Why would they? It's nobody's business."

"Garrett, please understand. I've told you before, there are rules of behavior and I just broke the first one. The dean would be angry about this, you know. You are my student, and we must remember that."

"But I thought we were friends?"

"Yes we are, dear."

Alex instantly regretted using an affectionate term, for it only confused him.

"Don't be hurt, Garrett. We do share a fine friendship. We talk together, we cook together. But we must keep our relationship professional, understand?"

"I didn't realize. Maybe I should take my tea to-go."

Alex looked at him and saw the little boy inside begging for Mom's approval. Unruly hair plastered down with dampness, his eyes searching hers for just the right answer. How she wanted to hug him, as she had David over the years, reassuring the child—the man-to-be—that he was indeed wonderful. But, of course, she didn't dare.

"Now that you're here, sit down and dry off. It's okay this once. And by the way, when we're not in class you don't have to call me 'Chef.'"

Garrett grinned as he sank into a chair and waited for a cup of companionship. "Would it be all right to call you Ms. S.?"

Alex smiled.

By a happy coincidence there was a stash of peanut butter cookies in the freezer. Alex took several out to defrost, but Garrett insisted they'd taste just fine for immediate consumption.

"I send cookies to my son at his university. He's on the East Coast."

"I didn't know you had a son, or anything—except that you were a star on TV."

"Hardly a star. Maybe a glimmer for a while." The casual remark, beginning with, of all things, cookies, built a bond neither could have foreseen. It began on a rain-swept afternoon when two generations with little in common sat in a kitchen, sharing dreams and regrets.

Words tumbled out easily, as though they needed to escape their long confinement. Alex spoke of ending a "forever" marriage, of her anxiety entering the business world, and of the sudden need to support herself. She talked about finding a new confidence and the courage to go forward, not knowing where or if she would land safely.

Garrett listened without interruption, even allowing a half-eaten cookie to remain. When Alex seemed finished, when all she'd been withholding had burst out, Garrett grasped her hand, conveying by touch what language could not. His empathy was real, for he, too, had traveled a difficult journey.

Unwanted and poorly cared for by a dismissive teenage mother, he had nearly raised himself, relying only on his determination to have a life, to be somebody decent. Whatever his haphazard genetics, he did get a nice face and exceptional intelligence. A youth counselor had suggested he apply to the Northridge College scholarship program, and to his astonishment he was awarded full academic and housing benefits. He only went back to the projects to see his mother when she called him for money. Working nights and weekends at a gas station, he bought a secondhand car, and he even had a credit card, which he kept secret from her.

"But I'm sure she cares about you. She gave you a great name."

"Yeah, she heard it in a movie about some dude with a beard who had to go fencing to defend his castle. She goes for that kind of stuff. My name? It's the only gift she's ever given me. Like I said, I only see her when I have to."

Alex sat silently; she needed to think this through. "You know, Garrett, she gave you the best of all gifts. She pushed you out of the nest and made you fly. Look where you are today. Look where you can be tomorrow."

He studied her expression, deliberating whether the advice given would become advice taken. Taking a deep breath, Garrett stood up, looked at his watch, and said it was time to leave.

"Take the cookies with you." Alex began filling a plastic bag. With a broad grin on his face, he grabbed the half-eaten one from his plate and, spinning around, shouted, "Thanks, Mom!" as he headed for the door. Alex, who could not mobilize her clumsy boot, stood staring after him, silently replying, "You're welcome, son."

5

TED

Spring reluctantly arrived and brought a renewed vibrancy in the air. The blue orthopedic klutz was replaced by a welcomed grace in Alex's step. Class menus were adjusted to warm-weather appetites, with the hearty broths and flavorful beef stews being replaced by lighter selections: salads from the sea served with fresh fruit short-cakes smothered with clouds of sweet cream.

The students enjoyed expanding their repertoire. Alex had deliberately curtailed her involvement with Garrett, asking an assistant to check his work. It had been foolish of her to accept his ride home and, in front of her neighbors, invite him in. Fortunately, no one called the dean to report her. But the experience was too precarious to repeat.

Garrett seemed to understand. He no longer lingered after class, using the excuse that he needed to clock in at the garage. His work continued to show progress; indeed he was a gifted chef-to-be.

Call it an epiphany—or more likely desperation—but one morning in May, Alex had an idea. Days earlier she had attended a faculty meeting chaired by Dr. Benneton. He requested a year-end review, including a financial statement. The culinary arts program, while accomplishing creative goals, was not profitable. After all the previous investments in equipment and continual purchasing, tuition had not compensated for expenditures. They were on the edge of trouble. The board of regents would not be patient. Something had to be done.

The dean walked Alex to her car, hoping to reassure her that her position was not yet in jeopardy; they'd find a solution. But he was an unconvincing actor. It was evident, even as he spoke words of confidence, that he was not hopeful.

Alex drove home that evening feeling the pressure. She could not lose this job. She could not start over again, worrying continually about money.

She slept fitfully, awakening often that night and the nights that followed, thinking over expenses and how to make cuts. But the results were unyielding. That's when the light bulb came on: she'd make a phone call to the best entrepreneur in the business, Ted Hudson. If anyone could brainstorm this problem, it would be him. Never once would she admit to herself how she longed to hear him say hello.

Where had she put his number? Yes, it was there, written on a slip of paper at the bottom of her jewelry box. Folded and left untouched for so many years, safely residing among her valuables. *What time would it be in Boca Raton now? Could I catch him on the golf course where he'd probably be?* Her hand felt rigid holding the phone. The pounding vibrations inside her warned of the risk, alerting her to be on guard. What if his wife was nearby? Would he be angry that she had imposed after all these years, and hang up brusquely? Maybe he wasn't alone and would be embarrassed to hear from a woman he'd long forgotten. Or—just perhaps—he would again be the man she had once loved so dearly.

Alex clutched the phone and listened as it rang for the

fourth time. *Please, please answer. I cannot leave a message, and I may not have the courage to call again.*

And then: "Alex, is that you? I saw it was you, and I couldn't believe it! How are you, how have you been?" His words were flustered, but his voice was warm and welcoming.

"Oh, Ted, it's so good to hear your voice." That was it: one restrained sentence. Alex knew she would ruin it all by allowing her feelings to tumble freely.

"Tell me, Alex, what are you doing now? You're still the best damn cook I ever met! I hope you're doing something creative."

"Yes, Ted, I'm an associate professor at Northridge College. Remember, it's about a half hour from the Culinary Arts Center —near the river?"

"Yes, I know that. It's got a fine reputation—and now a better one that you're on staff."

"Well, that's why I'm calling. We need help."

"You need money?"

"How did you know?"

Ted laughed and replied, "Because I've been in business a long time, darling. It always equates to dollars. So what's going on?"

Alex relaxed and poured the whole problem into Ted's lap: how her position could be canceled, how the dean was under pressure, and what in the world could they do to save the program—including her talented protégé, Garrett?

Ted listened intently. Alex pictured him drumming his forefinger on the desk, staring into space as though nothing else existed.

"Listen, Alex, I've got to give this more thought—but off the top of my head, why don't you utilize this genius kid as your personality and build around him? Promote a product and pitch him on your ads. What's his name, again?"

"Garrett. He works part-time as a mechanic when he's not cooking."

"So start a snack shop or a bakery or anything that brings in revenue."

"We could do that. Even a little restaurant on campus—"

Ted interrupted. "– And call it Garrett's Garage—just like I did with you, Alexandra the Grate, and it worked!"

"Oh, Ted, you are brilliant. I'll talk to the dean right away and see what we can pull together. Thank you for the ideas."

"Alex, there's a lot more to work through. Nothing's easy. Like I said, give me time to think and I'll get back to you. What's your email?"

Alex blurted out her answer, trying hard to sound calm even though she wanted to shout to the stratosphere. Ted was there for her; he still cared.

"Listen, I've got to run, but I don't want you to worry. This will work out, so take it easy."

"Bye, Ted, and thanks. You've been a great help."

"Good talking to you, beautiful."

The call ended. Alex stood very still, basking in the glow of his compliment. She hadn't expected him to remember. The special way he'd speak that word always made her feel beautiful. In a rush of sentiment, she was again enfolded in his arms, holding tight to all she could not release.

6

GARRETT'S GARAGE

Within the week Alex had formulated a concept. There would be options to choose: if Plan A didn't work, they could try Plan B or continue to Q if they had to. Dr. Benneton, at first skeptical, was coming around, encouraged by Amelia, who assured him that the hungry young students would be enthused. Now Alex had to convince Garrett to be the face of the sprouting enterprise.

"Oh, man, I don't know. I've never talked to people before. What did you call it—PR? What's that?"

"Public relations, Garrett. This will be your baby—Garrett's Garage! Dr. Benneton located an available space for us. It's in a campus warehouse, and we can use it for free. All we need to do is clean it up and decorate it like a garage. You know, tires on the walls, maybe pictures of vintage cars and an old convertible in the entrance as guests approach. Come on, Garrett, this is a chance for the community to find out about you—about what a great chef you are. You'll be helping the culinary arts program, too."

"Was it hard for you to be Alexandra the Grate on television?"

"Yes it was. I felt shy like you. But someone I trusted reached out to help me, and it brought me this job today."

Garrett groaned. His mouth contorted sideways as he deliberately avoided his mentor's eyes. Alex did not move. It was apparent that if she said one more word, if she pushed one more inch, he would close down and walk away. After an agonizing interlude, he sighed in resignation and reluctantly smiled. "You got a deal, Ms. S." Alex wanted to give him a hug, but settled for a firm handshake.

The next step was a large one: Dr. James Benneton, with all his savvy, would have to make a convincing presentation to the board of regents and win the endorsement of Dr. Anne Whitman, the college president.

The latter came first. She gave her approval after one meeting.

"How did you do it, Dr. Benneton? What did you say to convince her?" Alex asked incredulously.

As the dean smiled, a twinkle lit his face. "Well, I said, 'Annie I've got an idea you're going to like.'"

"You didn't!"

"Yes I did. Dr. Whitman and I go back many years—all the way to graduate school. We've spent a good amount of time together and shared a few drinks. She trusts me. My judgment. That's all there was to it. She'll send a recommendation to the board so ... " and as his voice trailed off, Alex understood his message.

Now that approval was secured, money became the next obstacle. The solution soon followed. It was nearly ten o'clock and Alex was getting ready for bed; she had an early conference in the morning. Water gushing from the faucet nearly drowned out the ringing phone. With suds dripping down her face, she answered the cell to hear Ted's hello.

"Sorry if I called late, Alex, but I needed to tell you something important." Before she could even reply he continued.

"I've arranged with my attorney to send you some cash flow—start-up capital for your project. Consider it a gift for a charitable cause."

"Oh, Ted, how thoughtful of you!"

"Well, it won't be enough, but it will get you started with a stove."

"It'll buy more than a stove for us."

"I'll cut a check from my business account and have Mac send a direct deposit to your account. I need that number at your bank. I can't write you a personal check because Jean would see it on our bank statement and wonder why the hell I'm sending money to a college in a city we left years ago. It wouldn't make sense to her."

"Well, she couldn't connect me."

"You're forgetting the internet, Alex. It would be easy to check the faculty—and she'd see your name. I don't want to start that suspicion again with all those questions she constantly asked. With technology today there's no privacy. Listen, this is the way I want it, so give me your account number."

Alex recited the numerals from memory, having called the bank so frequently to inquire about her dwindling balance.

"Good, we're all set. Best of luck, Alex. We'll keep in touch." And he was gone. Ted sounded tired. It wasn't usual for him to be abrupt. Alex tried to let it go; his intentions were generous, though tonight his manner was not.

Within days her checking account had swelled by two thousand dollars, courtesy of a deposit from the law office of MacNamara and Flynn, Boca Raton, Florida.

Ted was right: his contribution, although generous, was not enough to cover initial expenses. Even flea market tables and chairs cost money. Alex sat down with the dean, and together they made a laundry list of expenses—including the laundry itself. Soap, towels—every item had to be included.

"We can't make it. Even with our base, we're too short."

"Alexandra, don't let me hear you talk that way. We've got to make it. You know, Jack and I have been together for many years. We've gained some good investments over time. I'm able to put in the deficit to cover—"

"No, that's your money."

"Alex, it was Jack's idea. He's behind this venture all the way. He'll be angry if we don't go forward."

Alex didn't know if she should cry or laugh. She did neither, opting instead to say a soft "Thank you both" as she reached out to the dean, touching his arm gently.

Fortunately, the semester had ended, releasing time to the Garrett's Garage enterprise. For each hurdle crossed, others arose. Alex hunted down used restaurant supplies, getting lucky on finding an almost-new barbeque oven, perfect for the menus she had in mind. That was the next priority: food. What to serve, when to prepare, and how much to charge for it.

Garrett would be contributing his skill, but they would need more cooks in the kitchen. Tommy and Georgio, hoping to return to class as Alex's assistants for fall semester, readily agreed to work. "We'll both be there. Maybe alternate nights, but you can count on us." One spoke, the other nodded in agreement.

Alex knew to keep the menu simple: a few items well created and consistent. She suggested smoky chicken wings with buttermilk ranch dressing and pulled pork smothered in secret sauce.

"What's so secret about our sauce?" Garrett looked puzzled.

"It's such a secret I don't even know it yet! But I'll come up with something." Alex shook her head in disbelief. There she was, back in time, leaning over a barbeque grate to flavor a slab of meat.

"We can serve it with cornbread muffins and a garden coleslaw. Maybe add beans baked with brown sugar and bacon, too." Alex assured everyone that these foods would be easy and cost effective so profits should be good. Enthusiasm was contagious, and Garrett, over his initial reticence, was catching the fever.

Jack surprised the crew by showing up one day with cans of paint and brushes for all. An accomplished artist himself, he instructed anyone with a free hour to coat the walls with electric colors, adding his personal graphic mural of a Mercedes-Benz across the back of the room. It was the first visual guests would see as they entered the room. He also suggested they attach whitewall tires along the entranceway so oversized color photos of the foods could be inserted into the centers, tempting appetites.

As Alex returned to the kitchen area, she noticed a filled Mason jar on the counter with a note attached, reading, "This is my mother's recipe for bread-and-butter pickles. I would be honored if I could make them for the Garage." Signed, James Benneton. The gesture was so sweet, so sincere, that Alex called him immediately.

"Oh, Dr. Benneton, thank you for the offer. But the Health Department insists we make everything here on site."

"Then I shall come in after hours and produce them for you. I asked Jack to bring a sample just in case you didn't like them and would be too embarrassed to tell me."

"They're delicious, and we'll serve them proudly! The flavor will blend perfectly with our meals. Thanks."

Alex smiled for the rest of the day, envisioning the learned scholar, sleeves rolled up, diligently slicing cucumbers in tribute to his mother.

With the assistance of friends, former students and even interns, the grand opening finally arrived. Amelia collected a crew to place flyers on the windshields of every parked car on campus. Word of mouth circulated, and a notice went up on Facebook.

But without resources for citywide publicity, the opening threatened to be the closing. There was fierce competition that night from a big-name rock band at City Center. A ball game had also been scheduled, along with usual weekend attractions.

A handful of familiar appetites arrived early, but by seven p.m. most of the tables were still empty. The waitstaff, so eager, stood anxiously peering outward in hopes of seeing customers approach. They mingled in groups, trying to disguise their disappointment by joking, but their laughter was forced.

Alex had calculated running the restaurant three evenings a week, Friday through Sunday. If successful, they could always add hours. But to begin with, the weekends would yield sufficient profit. That is, if they had capacity crowds.

"At this rate, both the Garage and the culinary program are down the drain." Garrett's face was so somber as he said this Alex had to look away.

Valuable food was given away to the homeless that night, instead of selling to hungry patrons. Dean Benneton and President Whitman sat at one of the only occupied tables, talking quietly so no one could overhear. But Alex grasped their conversation and what the outcome would be if she didn't think of a quick fix. What would Ted do in this situation? How would he move mountains? Since that late-night call when he'd offered the money, Alex had not heard from him. What they once shared had faded into the sweetness of long ago, moments in a time she would not, could not, recapture. It was presumptuous to send a note or photos via his attorney. Dignity was imperative. Alex realized the only thing to do was nothing.

Reluctantly the staff began to leave; there was no sense just standing around waiting for customers who were enjoying themselves somewhere else. Even Dr. Benneton got up from his table, leaving a tip large enough for many to share. He escorted

President Whitman to the door, waving good night to anyone who cared to look his way.

Garrett and a few others readied the kitchen for the next night, hoping it would be more successful. Alex observed from the doorway how his shoulders had slumped down. His head, nearly as low, conveyed defeat.

"Garrett, this was only the first night. Business will improve. You'll see." But as she spoke the words, Alex wondered how she could make them come true. Garrett's Garage was closed until tomorrow. What miracle would she have to pull out of her Cuisinart to save it?

There was no pretending to sleep. Alex went through the ritual of tossing and turning, but all she gained were tangled sheets. She had once heard that it was better to get up and read until feeling drowsy, so she grabbed the first book that fell off the shelf. There was her miracle: a compilation of her television shows. Recipes, pictures of the set, letters from fans, and even an intro by the station's CEO. Photos of the friends she'd worked with smiled from the pages. Alex couldn't believe it had actually taken a book falling on her head to realize how the station could help. She'd call first thing in the morning. But for now, her eyelids finally felt heavy.

By nine a.m., after consuming a half pot of very strong coffee, Alexandra Silvers got to work. She phoned, she emailed, she texted. She did everything but stand on the corner, ringing a bell and shouting her requests. Most of the same staff were still at the station. She knew them to be compassionate people (even if they were artistically temperamental). Every one of them offered to help. By noon that day there were spot announcements about Garrett's Garage running multiple times an hour. All gratis, as community-service ads.

"Always happy to support a worthwhile project; makes our station look good, too," Ed Bassinger, the owner, exclaimed.

Alex quickly called Garrett, who in turn initiated a chain

response among the crew. That Saturday afternoon every TV on campus was turned to one single channel. Ed was right: a good deed is also good for business.

What a difference a day of advertising made! By five o'clock cars began filling the parking lot. An hour later, with no more space available, groups of customers crowded the sidewalk, hungrily inhaling the aromas of spicy meats emerging from the barbeque ovens. Garrett grabbed a tray and filled it with chunks of warm cornbread smothered in maple butter. Nearly dancing through the impatient crowd, he offered samples to the outstretched arms engulfing him and grinned at the repeated declarations of "Delicious."

Inside the Garage was organized chaos. This being their first night of real activity, everyone on staff was beyond multitasking. Servers were plating their own orders, Alex was helping the line cooks—even Dr. Benneton stood at a counter opening pickle jars, while Jack, with tongs in hand, placed a generous portion on each plate.

"My God, we're going to run out!" Jack sounded frantic.

"No, don't worry, Jack. Remember our reserve in the basement. We'll bring that over tomorrow. Then we'll make more for next week."

Those patrons who minded waiting for a table requested takeout. Amelia was pulled off hostess duties to manage those orders. But her absence complicated seating arrangements. Two couples began arguing over who was entitled to the next open table. Voices intensified, and one of the men, obviously a former football player, towered over his opponent. The scene looked ominous. Garrett rushed over to stand between them and offered complimentary dinners to whoever relinquished the table. In a burst of conciliation the linebacker agreed, stepping away so that the other couple could be seated. Garrett took a deep breath and retreated to safer ground.

Pandemonium over, by ten o'clock the service was finished

—and so were the servers. Everyone on staff was happily exhausted as much by the shock of success as the activity.

Alex stood in the doorway, hugging anybody she could get her hands on. They had survived the crisis. Garrett's Garage would be open tomorrow and lots of tomorrows, assuring Dr. Benneton would continue his culinary arts program, and Alex would be there proudly beside him.

It was nearly midnight as she drove home, too tired to worry about the next evening's conquest. Alex couldn't help but think of Ted and how pleased he'd have been tonight. She hadn't realized how much she'd learned: he'd shown her how to grab on to success and run so fast failure couldn't catch up. If only she could tell him all it meant to her. Her fingers stiffened around the steering wheel as she attempted to clasp hard to reality. Above her, in a darkened sky, a burst of stars twinkled around the moon, tempting the night with possibilities.

Alex could scarcely navigate in the shadowy condo. She had left home in the brightest of hours and forgot to leave on a lamp. Somehow she maneuvered safely across the room to the nearest light switch, before securing herself into a chair. Her purse in her lap, she retrieved her phone and began touching the numbers with her right forefinger. The series was Ted's cell. She knew she could not continue. She could not press send. Admitting it was only a childish game, Alex reluctantly relinquished the phone into its leather case, sighed deeply, and fell into bed, exhausted.

The three-night restaurant continued to be popular, attracting guests from the entire city. Dean Benneton spent every Saturday morning at the farmers market, supporting the local cucumber growers. He bought everything they could harvest. Some smart kid dubbed him the Pickle Professor, and by midsummer the name had become a local moniker. The art department came up with a cartoon sticker: a pickle wearing a professorial mortarboard, available for one buck, proceeds donated to the Garrett's Garage project.

Alex was delighted with the restaurant's success and constantly impressed with Garrett's abilities. A skilled grill master, he seemed to sense when the meat was ready—charred on the outside, yet moist and tender. Thick slabs were so juicy the customers almost needed bibs. On nights when Tommy or Georgio could relieve him, Garrett improvised all the side dishes, using unusual combinations of marinated vegetables on beds of whole-grain rice. He dusted sweet potatoes with caramelized onions and deep-fried zucchini spears so crisp and crunchy that even children asked for seconds. His talent continued to expand. Where it emerged from would remain a mystery. Garrett revealed only that he watched the Food Network often during his lonely childhood.

Everyone nearly laughed when he apologized for the dessert tray. It contained only three items, but nobody expected more: a chocolate brownie crust spilling over with a frothy raspberry crème filling, brandied peaches served with home-made vanilla bean gelato, and mammoth sugar cookies along-side a mug of cold milk. Kids of all ages ordered that one.

Garrett was so quick that the others stepped back when they stood in his path. Everyone agreed: he was a young man to watch.

The TV station continued to run the ads, so business was steady—even on those steamy, sticky August nights when people insisted they were too hot to be hungry.

On most Saturday nights Charlie Coleman came by to entertain the crowd. Black silk shirt, black slacks—he made quite an impression and sounded marvelous even on a small keyboard. Sometimes a few of his students would come along to play their guitars, often joined by an aspiring vocalist. Guests never knew what entertainment to expect, which added to the fun. Alex was too busy to pay much attention, although it was obvious that Charlie upped the tempo whenever she was near.

It all seemed too good to be true—which of course, it was. On a particularly crowded Friday in late August, Alex was hosting at the front end when she heard Garrett's voice above the usual commotion. She couldn't decipher precisely what he was saying, but she knew something was wrong. Very wrong. Instructing the customers to seat themselves, she rushed into the kitchen to see Garrett thrashing his arms in agitation and speaking to—or shouting at—the couple confronting him.

"Ma, you shouldn't have come. You're embarrassing me. I work here—I can't give you free stuff. You'll get me in trouble!"

The woman was defiant, and refused to move, but the man with her started to laugh and grabbed for Garrett's arm.

"Hey, kid, what's it to you? A couple of dinners for the old folks. C'mon, Garrett, you owe us." He extended his arms as Garrett backed away. Alex was afraid one of them would actually lunge at the other. It was obvious neither was backing down. Luckily, before the first punch could land, one of the servers—the star of the wrestling team—came into the kitchen, saw the confrontation, and approached the trio, flexing his muscular arms.

"What's going on here?" he asked, although he knew the answer. Garrett regained his composure enough to reply, "Nothing, Brad, they were just leaving."

"That's good. We need you on the grill, Garrett. A couple of guys from campus police just drove up and placed a big order." Brad smiled, nodded to the couple, and told them goodbye. That's all it took. The woman turned to Garrett, muttering something about his giving her some money so they could go to McDonald's.

"I'm in work clothes, Ma. I don't have anything on me." But the piercing look in his mother's eyes seared through him.

"Wait here, I'll see what I got tonight." He turned sharply

toward the employees' area. His mother stepped forward to follow, but her companion grabbed her arm to hold her back.

"Give the kid a minute, Millie Mae, he'll come back." Restrained, she watched the doorway anxiously awaiting her son—and his money.

Alex now understood Garrett's background. From the paradox of his mother's ineptness he'd grasped an incentive to make something of the life begrudgingly given him. Because of his mother's weakness he'd gained the strength to claw his way from the depths and show the world—and himself—all he was worth.

Unaware that she was being analyzed, Millie Mae stood silent, though the twist of her shoulders shouted impatience. Years ago she might have been pretty; her deep-set eyes, reminiscent of her son's, might once have been bright with the promise of tomorrow, but too many hours after midnight and years of too little restraint had dimmed their shine. The dress, the shoes, the multitude of beaded jewelry were a pathetic display of someone trying too hard to look younger and less used.

In contrast, the man alongside her was fastidious in his plaid sport coat and fitted trousers. The silk hankie that protruded from his breast pocket matched his tie. He had more facial growth in a moustache and trimmed beard than he did slicked back on the top of his head. Though she kept her distance, Alex inadvertently inhaled a dose of his cologne. *How sad,* she thought, *these two people trying to be something, only to have lost their direction in the struggle.*

At that point Garrett reappeared, handed his mother the few bills he had, and nearly pushed them out the back door. As they turned to leave without looking back, Alex stood there in near disbelief. Garrett was beyond humiliation, so angry he was literally shaking. It was apparent he couldn't talk about what just happened. Belittled by his mother and some man she'd picked up on her way, they had come by to pressure him for handouts and had not a word of praise or a smile of support for this young protégé. Alex thought of her own David, who had enjoyed a life filled with kindness and opportunities. Grateful for one son and heartbroken for the other, she could only reach out to him and gently touch his shoulder. She wanted to hug him, to hold him close as she always had for David when he'd been hurting. But they were in a public arena, and such a gesture could be misinterpreted.

"Gotta get to the grill, Ms. S. Too busy to talk." With that announcement he brushed by her, deliberately avoiding her reply.

Garrett never brought up the incident—or his mother—again that summer. Perhaps by doing so he could erase it from his mind.

7

THE SAPPHIRE STAR

On schedule, Alex and Dr. Benneton met with the board of regents, beaming as they handed out their fiscal report. At least for the near future, the culinary arts program at Northridge College would continue. Countless students would have the chance to enter the food industry to become chefs and restaurateurs. With a renewed reputation, even out-of-state students had registered. Dr. Benneton could relax and Alex could count on her pension.

As the last summer warmth succumbed to the crispness of a crimson autumn, Alex was consumed by her workload. The restaurant would only be serving until the end of September, overlapping the first week of classes. That meant Alex had to finalize her curriculum between shifts overseeing the Garage. It gave her no time to even daydream of contacting Ted, and all thoughts of him were comfortably tucked away. For now.

Reviews for the restaurant had been good and the publicity constant, so it wasn't shocking when a food writer from the *Associated Press* picked up a favorable column from the local newspaper and ran it as a human-interest story nationally. It had such an unusual twist ("Restaurant Saves Culinary

Program") that Dr. Benneton's office was deluged with responses. Amelia had a friend come in to handle the overflow.

The article went into detail about Garrett. Alex couldn't have been more pleased. It also mentioned her, but most of all it showcased a young talent.

Soon after its publication, a call came into the dean's office. It was from an Alain Trebeau, New York. Amelia immediately put it through.

"Dean, you have a caller on line two. He wants to talk to you, but his accent is so heavy I could hardly understand him." With that she transferred the call, listening in ever so quietly.

"'Allo, Dean Benneton. I am executive chef at ze Sapphire Star Hotel in New York."

That was all Amelia dared listen to, lest her breathing could be heard on the extension. Turned out, it wasn't necessary to eavesdrop. Within minutes Dr. Benneton burst out of his office as though he'd been launched through space. Amelia jumped up, ready to grab him if he fell over.

"What is it?"

"That call. It was that famous chef from New York. He's read about us. Why we opened a restaurant and all about Garrett." The dean paused to catch his breath—which was a good thing because his face had turned bright red.

"He's heard about us and what?" Amelia was nearly shouting from the suspense.

"He wants Garrett to come to New York and work for him at the hotel!"

If a dignified dean and his young assistant could be caught embracing, this was their moment. Amelia had to stop herself from jumping up and down.

"I've got to tell Alex. I'll let her give him the news." With that, the dean bounded back into his office to place the jubilant call.

Garrett quickly became the news du jour. Everyone seemed

to know within the hour. Most of the restaurant crew were delighted. A few, of course, were jealous and felt it should have been them. But the majority planned a big celebration for the following week. Alex was asked to host, and Dr. Benneton would be the master of ceremonies. All Garrett could say was "Wow!" It was the chance of his lifetime.

When the hoorays had quieted, a somber thought occurred to Alex. She had never asked Garrett about money—or lack thereof. She worried how he would initially survive in such an expensive city. How could he even buy plane fare to get there in the first place? He'd be unable to make payments on his Visa card. All these questions were on her mind when she went to meet him for coffee at a little café near campus.

Garrett was already waiting in a back booth, away from the commotion. His face beamed with good news. Alex slid in across from him, eager to hear what he couldn't wait to say.

"What is it, Garrett? You look like you're ready to explode!"

Garrett smiled, teasing for a moment before he began. "Well, you know, Ms. S., you've been talking about my expenses in New York, and where the money would come from. I was worried too—until I stopped to think."

"Stopped to think what?"

"That I had this old bank account from when I was a kid."

"Go on, I'm listening."

"Ever since I started school I put something into a savings account. Everybody in class did, I think on Tuesdays. The teacher handed out these envelopes and each kid brought whatever money they had to deposit. It all went into the neighborhood bank, Northwinds State. I did this all the way through with whatever I'd earned, whatever jobs I could find that week. I was saving for a lot of years, but I shoved it to the back of my mind so I wouldn't be tempted to spend any of it. I needed the security of knowing I had money there waiting for me just in case."

Alex sat motionless, concentrating on Garrett's expression. He continued.

"Let me explain this so you really understand. Cuz you've never been totally broke. I mean so down that mud oozed through your shoes cuz they were so torn up. Well, it's not a lot —two thousand, three hundred and fifty-seven dollars. But in my mind it was the barrier between me and the damn mud. I *never* want to feel that slime again!"

Alex could only nod in response. Garrett's tone brightened. He even grinned as he described emptying his closet to pack. "The deposit book nearly fell on my head. For years it's been pushed back on a shelf. When I opened it, I was so relieved. I have plenty to get me to New York and be okay until those paychecks start coming,"

Alex didn't have to say congratulations. Garrett was ecstatic beyond words. Instead she ordered two chocolate mocha lattés with whipped cream so that they could appropriately toast to his future success.

Engrossed in conversation, Garrett glanced at his watch and noted that the afternoon was flying and he should get to the bank soon. "I really don't want to go back to the old neighborhood. But I guess it'll be okay. I'll say goodbye to all that for the last time."

His voice trailed off, but Alex knew what he meant: to all that unhappiness. The two left the coffee shop, pleased to continue on their way.

As usual, Alex had errands to do before arriving at the Garage for dinner service. Within minutes of her arrival, Amelia approached her to ask if she'd seen Garrett in the last hours.

"Why? What's wrong?" Call it intuition, but Alex sensed an immediate apprehension. *What could have happened in four hours?*

"Well, Garrett's always here early to do prep, and nobody's

seen or heard from him." Amelia nervously peered across the room, hoping her absent chef might be hiding behind the display counter.

As minutes evolved into an hour and guests began to arrive, Garrett's mysterious disappearance magnified.

Where can he be? He's never done this before escalated into *Maybe something's happened to him!*

One of the servers who had just come on duty remembered he had Garrett's cell number and offered to call.

"Why didn't you tell us before!" scolded Amelia. "We're standing here, frantic!"

"Sorry, I'll try right now." He grabbed the phone tapping the numbers nervously, and let it ring until voicemail picked up. The others caught his expression, knowing immediately there had been no response.

"So now what should we do?" asked another server.

"Wait and hope," was all Alex could reply.

The evening continued, not as usual but as necessary. There was no sign of the missing Garrett. Repeated calls and attempted messages did not get through. Someone even went over to his apartment, but the manager said he hadn't been home. It was nearly closing. Alex was about to begin calling hospitals when suddenly the back door was thrust open and a very inebriated Garrett appeared. It was all he could do to stagger into the kitchen and fall onto the nearest chair. Head down, his hands nearly covering his face, Garrett just sat there breathing deeply from his chest—almost groaning as he exhaled. As Alex approached, she was nearly overwhelmed with the stench of alcohol he emitted. She reached over to him prying each finger away, shocked to feel the moistness of tears.

"Garrett, what on earth happened? What have you done?" But there was no reply. Only a sigh, more like a whimper.

Again Alex questioned him. Not until a third attempt did

she begin to break through, although his response was barely audible.

"She stole it, all of it. Right away from me."

"What are you talking about? Who stole what? Who is she?" Alex persisted.

"Ma—and Morris. He put her up to this. I know that cuz she's not smart enough to do it herself. My money. She stole all of it."

Alex put her arms around his, but it was too late to shield him from the dreadful reality. By this time he was shuddering —not from chill but with grief.

"Start from the beginning, dear. Tell me from the start what's happened." Alex shooed the collection of curious onlookers out of the room (although she knew they would be listening nearby).

Garrett began, "You know that savings account I was just telling you about? Well, I forgot Ma was cosigner. I was just a kid, and she had to have her name listed too. The bank insisted but I made sure the statements came to me. I never would have figured it, but Ma and Morris came to my place a few days ago pretending they wanted to say goodbye. I wasn't home and my roommate, not suspecting anything, let them into our room so Ma could leave me a note. All they really wanted was to hit me up for cash before I left town. Well, Morris must have spied the Northwinds State envelope on my desk and grabbed it. He called the bank and asked if Ma could withdraw the money. They said, 'Yes, she was the cosigner and it would be valid.' So that's what happened. He told her he'd buy her a fancy diamond necklace and take her to Florida next winter and she believed him. All she had to do was go to the bank and close out the account. She swore to me she argued with him but he convinced her the money really belonged to her for all the expense I'd cost her growing up. So that's it. The money's gone, and so is my chance for New York."

Alex thought it incomprehensible, a hellish scheme no parent should ever inflict. There were gasps from behind the door. His humiliation would be public.

Garrett struggled up from the chair and slammed his fist against a cabinet with such force the wood cracked. In pain, he bellowed language so obscene that Alex turned away with trepidation. Two or three of the male servers rushed into the room to subdue him before he hurt someone—or himself. Demanding that he calm down did no good. Finally, the explosiveness within him and the saturation of alcohol worked together, and he plummeted to the floor to sleep off his rant.

For half a moment Alex thought of calling Millie Mae and chastising her. But she knew it would do no good. The money was gone—as was that woman's conscience.

With only weeks left, they needed to think quickly. Two thousand, three hundred and fifty-seven dollars can be a king's fortune when no one has it. Garrett had to get to his new job. The Indigo Room at the Star Sapphire Hotel was waiting.

Fearful of asking too much, Alex hesitated to call the TV station to request another favor, but with Dr. Benneton's encouragement she relented.

"I'm embarrassed to impose, Mr. Bassinger, but you see we have this problem." She reiterated the situation, and to her relief her plea was received with interest and compassion. They would hold a Get Garrett Going night in the parking lot of the station: a ten-dollar-a-head fundraiser featuring brats and beer and entertainment by the Campus Rockers. All this to be organized and completed within two weeks. The entire Garage crew volunteered to help serve. Dr. Benneton's office staff, headed by Amelia, took over sales and food and beverage supplies. Alex worked with her former associates at the station to publicize the event.

Garrett couldn't believe people were being so nice to him. "I can't get it through my thick head that so many people would help a nobody kid like me."

At first Alex reassured him that he was indeed worthwhile. But after his third expression of self-doubt she gave up trying to convince him. He'd soon see his value for himself.

Between campus chatter and the media exposure, the Get Garrett Going event was overwhelming. Although most everyone attending was pleased to contribute to a good cause, the majority seemed more enthused about having fun. Dr. Benneton proved himself to be an expert master of ceremonies, displaying a wry humor seldom seen in the classroom. Jack auctioned off three still lifes, and Alex offered "Dinner for Eight catered by Yours Truly." Those items, plus a few others, brought in enough to sustain Garrett's first weeks in New York.

Plane ticket secured, suit and tie for interview tailored to fit and paid for, reservations made for his first two weeks' lodging, all was in order. The difficult part, the piece no one wanted to put in place, was the letting go.

The class met at the campus coffeehouse, thinking a public farewell would be less emotional. The theory was good, but some of the girls got a bit teary. It was a bittersweet moment, for they had shared much together. The guys, all Garrett's bros during these past years (and especially this summer), stood around awkwardly. Not wanting to show sentiment or, in their estimation, get "mushy," they feigned a lightheartedness to disguise their true feelings. Everyone, young and old, was delighted for Garrett's opportunity. But that meant parting with a friend and they'd miss him more than they realized.

After all the embraces and promises to keep in touch, when there was no other reason to remain together, each person drifted in their separate direction.

Garrett saved Alex for his final goodbye. As she reached out to him, he suddenly dropped his head down on her shoulder—reminiscent of a child parting from the security of its mother.

Alex, overcome with the pure sweetness of his gesture, softly whispered to him. "You'll be just fine. I will be here whenever and forever, for you." Then, just as spontaneously, he turned away and walked out the door, never looking back. Alex knew it was not out of callousness. Quite the opposite. She was the first woman he had loved. She had taught him how to care. About others. About himself.

The last of the group disbanded. Alex stopped on her way home to buy groceries she didn't need. Anything to stall before opening the door to a lonely condo.

8

GOOD TIME CHARLIE

F all semester opened as the Garage door closed. There was talk of next year's restaurant, but it was too soon to plan; much would happen before that. Culinary classes were filled to capacity with ambitious students competing for both attention and the deep fryer. Though there wasn't a potential Garrett, many were capable and anxious to learn. Alex and her two assistants had a daily challenge to keep one sauce ahead of them. It was exhausting and she soon spent her weekends recuperating—sometimes sleeping late on a Saturday.

One particular morning was different, being interrupted by the persistent ringing of her phone.

"Who dares to bother me in the middle of the night?" Alex grumbled without glancing at the wall clock. She grabbed the source of her annoyance, growled "Hello," and waited for the intruder to respond.

"Alex, is that you? This is Charlie Coleman. I must have disturbed you."

Partially awake now, Alex managed a civil "Sorry, Charlie, I was sleeping in. This semester is so demanding and I try to rest up when I can."

"I hear what you're saying! Especially after your hectic summer with the restaurant. That reminds me, have you heard from Garrett?"

"Yes, he keeps in close touch. The executive chef put him on the line. He started with salad prep, but next week he'll be adding soups, too. He's working hard—and long. But he's never sounded happier."

"I'm sure he'll always be grateful to you."

"Garrett's a good kid. He'd have gone far on his ability."

"Alex, speaking of going far, how about dinner tonight? There's a new place downtown I've heard good things about ..."

To her own surprise, Alex heard herself accepting.

"See you at seven." Charlie's response was equally spontaneous. He hadn't thought it would be this easy; Alex had always been so nonchalant, on the edge of disinterested, and he had braced himself for rejection. He was delighted to hear the reply he'd hoped for.

Promptly at seven that evening, Charlie Coleman pressed a doorbell allowing him entrance to the world of a woman he'd long admired.

Perhaps it was the remedial rest of that morning—or the buoyant flattery of a man's attention—but that evening Alexandra looked marvelous. Her dark hair, swept back from her face, allowed the warmth of her eyes to charm anyone within view. The intense activity of the past months had stimulated her metabolism—resulting in less cushioning—so her black silk sheath slid luxuriously over trim hips.

Conversation in the car was sporadic. Either they chatted nervously, sometimes interrupting each another, or there was complete silence. It was evident that Charlie was trying to make an impression, and it amused Alex that a man of his age and achievements wouldn't feel more confident.

The restaurant was packed to capacity with people trying to

squeeze their way through the narrow entrance. A young man
wearing a white dinner jacket stood guard by a long velvet cord,
appeasing everyone anxious to be seated. Although Charlie
had made a reservation, their table was not yet available as the
present diners lingered over their dessert liqueurs. To compensate for the delay they were offered a complimentary drink at
the bar—which they readily accepted. No sooner had they
ordered when Charlie felt a less-than-gentle slap on his back.
He turned to see a balding man, dressed in a navy sports coat,
extending his hand as he smiled warmly.

"Gus, how the hell are you and what are you doing here?"
Before the question could be answered, two other men, both
wearing similar jackets, appeared. Charlie knew them, too. The
foursome got into quite a conversation before there was an
opportunity to introduce Alex. Musician friends of many years,
the trio was playing in the dining room on weekend nights.

"After the break, why don't you sit in for a set, Charlie?
There is a good piano—and we'll just improvise." Gus turned
to Alex as if to convince her and, pointing to Charlie, added,
"Best keyboard man in town!"

Before Alex could nod approval, Charlie broke in. "Some
other time, Gus. We're here for dinner tonight. I'll just sit back
and listen."

Gus got the hint, and after polite goodbyes, the trio headed
for the main room where their instruments were waiting.

Alex was impressed with their comradery and admiration
of Charlie. She knew he was well respected as an associate
professor, but she hadn't realized his reputation to others as an
outstanding musician.

Their table was finally open and dinner was served, but not
enjoyed. Although Charlie didn't seem to notice, Alex struggled
with the dry, overcooked chicken and potatoes fried in used oil.
It was obvious that the club didn't care about haute cuisine and
focused on profitable liquor sales instead. This was not a place

to which she'd return. Charlie apparently didn't care, concentrating on his friends. He was totally enthralled with their music. It was too loud to converse, so they could only speak between numbers.

Charlie had ordered a bottle of wine to toast Garrett's success, but even that was interrupted by Gus's intrusive announcement: "Tonight we're privileged to have a great talent with us. Folks, let's bring him up here with a round of applause. Charlie Coleman, everyone!"

Alex looked at Charlie. He looked back with a *What can I do?* expression and, almost jumping out of his chair, mouthed the words *I'll be right back* before rushing toward the piano. After a thirty-second conference the newly formed quartet opened with an R'n'B favorite, to the crowd's boisterous approval. Alex realized she had lost him to a roomful of fans. As the hour passed and the intensity of rhythm increased, the audience wouldn't allow him to stop. Charlie was home, loving every minute of the music—and adoration.

Alex sipped her glass of wine, making a silent and solitary salute to Garrett. She wasn't quite sure which of two choices she should make next: remain at the table alone or wave to Charlie as she got up to leave. He was so absorbed she wasn't sure he'd even notice. Taxis frequented the street outside, and with a credit card tucked in her purse, it would be easy. But did she really want to go? To walk away from this excitement? Nevertheless, being deserted at a table was embarrassing. Imagined or not, she felt glaring eyes descend upon her singular silhouette.

Alex pushed back her chair, and, just as she rose, the music ended. Everyone around her, assuming she was encouraging a standing ovation, also stood up and began applauding. The four musicians bowed in response, turning to Alex in appreciation. She had no choice but to stand still and wait until Charlie returned to the table. When he did, he grabbed her and kissed her with much enthusiasm. It was all so spontaneous that Alex could only smile at those who watched approvingly. Charlie then motioned to the waiter for the check and, as soon as it was paid, announced, "We should get out of here."

All the way to the door, even while waiting for their car, people came up to him—praising, asking for an autograph. Alex stood to the side, watching, as Charlie enjoyed their attention.

On the drive home he was high on the adrenaline of success. Alex was tired, and it was nice to just listen to his glowing commentary. As he walked her to her door, Alex debated for one second about inviting him in for a nightcap. But he was already sufficiently intoxicated with the stimulation of the evening. No, she would say thank you and goodnight, and that would be all.

Charlie leaned closer, hoping to read a message in her eyes. But there was none. If he felt disappointed, he didn't show it, instead giving her a quick kiss somewhere in the vicinity of her mouth. He then turned toward his car with a standard salutation of "I'll call you." Whether he meant it or not, Alex wasn't sure.

Two weeks went by. A third began. Alex maintained her usual hectic pace, but between classes, on the way to a meeting, as she drove home, her thoughts drifted to Charlie—or rather the lack of him. The hours they'd spent together propelled through her mind. He hadn't seemed to notice her disappointment at having to share him with the entire room. Maybe that was his standard procedure, leaving his women alone at a table. Well, then, he was welcome to call his fans instead! All the while she knew her defensiveness was only a hollow attempt to make herself feel better. The reality was that he had let her down. He said he'd call, and he hadn't. Over and over again she analyzed what she had said or which gesture withheld to cause this disconnect. Was it a mistake not inviting him in? He should have realized it wasn't appropriate; they barely knew each other. Alex wondered if they ever would.

Another week passed with no Charlie. Was her frustration based solely on pride? He had, from the first, been so available. Now, suddenly, they'd changed lanes. They were too old, too experienced to be playing for the thrill of the chase. Somehow she needed closure.

Alex decided she had nothing to lose by calling. It would be best to leave a message between classes. That way he could respond at his convenience, when he had time to talk and explain himself.

Alex dialed as planned, but to her dismay she heard Charlie's "Hello" and realized she'd have to confront him right on.

In a voice too casual to be believed, she opened, with "Just thought I'd ask how you are."

"Glad you called, Alex, I've been thinking about you."

"And?"

"Well there's been something on my mind. This isn't a good time to go into it." Alex swallowed hard, bracing for negative news.

"Listen, rather than say too much now, why don't we meet for a drink later today? My last class finishes at four. How about the pub over on Sixth Street?"

"Fine. I'll do some desk work and see you then." She put down the phone and spent the ensuing hours wondering, even worrying, about what Charlie would say.

Though she assumed he'd be there waiting, Alex got to the pub before Charlie. Feeling self-conscious sitting alone, she ordered a cocktail for herself. By the time Charlie did arrive, her glass was half empty and she hoped it wasn't symbolic of their anticipated conversation.

"Sorry, I got detained. Hope you haven't been waiting long." Charlie was somewhat out of breath as he sank onto the high stool beside her.

Glib chatter followed just to fill the air. Nothing of importance—only a stall to avoid the inevitable reason they met. Finally, Charlie came round to the subject. Perhaps it was the bourbon that gave him the shot of courage.

"Alex, you've probably wondered why I haven't called these past weeks. I feel I owe you an explanation."

Alex insisted it wasn't necessary, but Charlie continued talking.

"Believe me, it wasn't because I didn't want to be with you again. Quite to the contrary but ..." His voice trailed off so suddenly that Alex had to ask him to repeat himself.

"To be honest, I felt you were only doing me a favor. You went along with my friends, my lifestyle, and well, to put it bluntly, we live in opposite worlds. Yours is neat and precise, while mine is all over the keyboard. I don't want to pull you into a place where you don't want to be."

"Charlie, I went out with you because I wanted to. Okay, I agree we're totally different. Up until now I've lived according to my recipes: carefully measured and predictable. Maybe it's time to dance to the music. I'm here today because I want to be. That's all I need to say!"

Alex stopped to take a breath—and to digest her own admission, which she blurted forth from somewhere she hadn't known existed. Maybe this was her answer at last. The past weeks of anxiety were not because of pride or vanity. In truth, she wanted more of a good thing called Charlie.

Flattered beyond expectation, Charlie gazed down at the table as if he'd just noticed the wood was inlaid with gold. When he finally looked up and saw Alex's expression, he took her hand in his as he smiled. Sweet as the moment was, Alex could not escape the truth: it wasn't Ted's smile.

With that discussion out of the way, the two new friends became old friends, so absorbed that they were startled when the overhead lights turned on, welcoming the night.

Alex reacted at once. "Look at the time; it must be well after six. I'd better get started home!"

"Why don't we grab a quick dinner first?"

"Oh, Charlie, I don't have time tonight. I've got to finish a report for Dr. Benneton."

Charlie nodded as if he understood, but Alex could see he really didn't.

"There you go again, letting that insecurity get you! Come for dinner this Saturday. I'll make something special."

For the second time that afternoon, Charlie smiled at Alex as though she was the loveliest woman in the universe. This time she returned his smile and took his arm, and together they walked to their separate cars.

Nothing seemed to go right. The salad dressing refused to blend smoothly, the fruit pie oozed over in the oven and, of course, the mashed potatoes had lumps. Alex felt as if she were back in seventh-grade Home Ec class, all thumbs. Maybe her anticipation of being alone with Charlie had traveled down to her hands as she dropped the napkins on the floor.

"This is silly—just juvenile," she chided herself. When the doorbell rang, she managed a quick once-over in the mirror before greeting her guest.

Charlie, in contrast, was his most relaxed. Dressed in slacks and a sweater, he clearly anticipated an evening of good food and conversation. And, Alex hoped, nothing more. Maybe that thought had provoked her tension. She wasn't ready to jump into bed on a casual date.

There was enough wine to make dinner flow smoothly. Charlie asked for seconds, not noticing the culinary imperfections Alex had fretted about. He devoured the food as if he hadn't enjoyed a home-cooked meal since leaving his mother's kitchen. Alex teased him that his basic nutrition came from the olives in a martini. He laughed but didn't disagree.

After disguising the deflated pie with ice cream, they settled contentedly in the living room. Charlie sprawled out on the couch, feet on an ottoman, and began, without provocation, to reminisce about years past.

"I've loved music ever since I can remember; the biggest influence was my grandparents' home. The sound of those vinyl recordings resonated throughout the house and captivated me. Really blew my mind." He was silent for a minute, enjoying the nostalgia of those early years.

His mother played enough piano to help him find middle "C." Before his hands could stretch an octave he knew what he'd do with his life. Of course, there were obstacles, such as his father, a man of no nonsense, unimaginative and opposed to his son's aspirations. "A pharmacist always makes a reliable living," he would announce with fervor. Charlie, assuming a somber tone, enunciated the words as if he'd heard each a thousand times. Alex sat quietly, listening, allowing him the emotional cleansing.

Charlie had won a partial scholarship to the prestigious American Music Conservatory and, while taking every booking he could get, from weddings to bar mitzvahs, managed to graduate with a coveted degree.

Although classically trained, he knew the direction his career would take him. Much to the annoyance of his father and the apprehension of his mother, he headed for New York and the Village jazz scene. Years of playing in clubs, touring the country with big names, and doing studio work on the coast finally exhausted his endurance, so on one sobering day he applied for—and was hired for—a teaching position at Northridge College. He had always liked the Midwest, and it seemed just the right antidote to a knocked-around life on the road he could no longer travel. His greatest regret was that his father didn't live long enough to see him settled.

Suddenly quiet, Charlie closed his eyes, and Alex wondered if all that soul searching had been too much (combined with pie a la mode). Timed passed them by while the two remained in the stillness of a faintly lit room. It was later than they realized when Charlie opened his eyes, looked at his watch, and startled himself upright.

"How did it get so late?" he asked, more as a statement than a question. "I'd better get going. I'm playing a brunch at the Women's Club tomorrow. Nice little ladies who tip well." He chuckled as he rose to his feet.

Alex took his hand as they walked to the door. She had worried for no reason; Charlie wasn't expecting to spend the night. "Good night," she said, "I'm glad you came over. We can do this again sometime."

Charlie gave her a hug and turned to leave. "Thanks, Alex. See you at school."

As she closed the door, she wondered if that had been his way of saying goodbye. Had he searched for—and not found—what he was looking for? "See you at school" was a strange way to end the evening.

Before she could turn the calendar page, autumn evolved into winter, unusually cold that year with frequent ice storms. Having learned the "Blue Boot Blues" from her ankle accident, Alex limited her activities around the city, quite content to spend leisure hours at home. But not alone.

Charlie did see her at school—and after hours, too. Alex teased him about showing up so often at mealtime. His slender frame became more attractive, and certainly healthier, with proper nutrition. After initial objections, he even condescended to eat fruits and vegetables, joking that he no longer depended on the citrus in sangria for his vitamin C.

Gradually, he stayed later and later into the evening, sometimes sleeping over when the weather restricted his driving. Alex was comfortable with that arrangement, and Charlie seemed as content.

They became dear friends and close confidants. She was his

Allie. They adapted to each other's moods, seeming to sense when to talk or be silent from tone of voice or the way the other walked into a room. They were loyal to a relationship no one else needed to understand. Each had withstood life's bruising and faced unique challenges, stumbling often on their journey to discover their own purpose.

Charlie was a tender and considerate lover, wrapping Alex in the warmth of his arms and whispering the sweet lyrics of a love song yet to be written. The melody from his heart to hers gave her moments to feel cherished. But he would never be Ted. The desire she had felt years before still smoldering in her memory, the embers relentlessly refusing to extinguish.

There were those nights, too, when Charlie would give Alex a quick kiss and be out before she could even turn out the light. Teaching days and playing gigs on the weekend was exhausting. But that was okay. When the howling wind mimicked fierce wolves on the hunt, when storms splattered against windowpanes, Alex felt secure lying beside him—with dreams of a long-ago love lingering as she slumbered.

9

DAVID

"Hey, Mom, start cooking! Your best customer is on his way."

"David, is this you?"

"Who else would it be, Mother!" Alex had been startled from a deep sleep by the phone's intrusive ring.

"David, you're calling so late. Is everything all right?"

"There you go again, Mom, always worrying about me. Everything's not all right—it's great! Actually, it's fantastic!"

"What are you talking about?"

"Well, sorry if I woke you, but this couldn't wait until morning. Dad just called from L.A. You know it's much earlier there. Anyhow, he wanted to clue me in before tomorrow. Get this, Mom, the office manager at his law firm will be calling me for a job opening. Their CFO is interviewing for a position in the accounting department, and he's interested in talking to me. I've already faxed him as much info as I could. I put together a résumé, and of course Dad said a few good words, too." David stopped to catch a breath before continuing. "He's been working out of that office while he supposedly vacationed in Palm Springs. It's not as big as the home office there, but still, there's a lot of attorneys and a good opportunity for me to assist their tax accountants. Anyhow, I'm to set up a meeting in L.A. as soon as possible. That'll give me a chance to stop by and see you on my way out. I'll set the whole thing up and call you in a day."

"But David, it's so close to graduation. Does this mean you'll miss commencement? I had my classes juggled, a plane ticket purchased, a hotel booked. Am I supposed to cancel all this and just take a loss? Won't you regret not wearing a cap and gown?"

"Mom, I did all that pomp-and-circumstance thing when I was an undergraduate. A master's degree is different. They can mail me my diploma. It's important I meet this CFO—grab the opportunity before someone else aces me out. Oh, and don't even think about the money thing. I'll reimburse you with my first paycheck."

Alex realized her son had called not to ask her opinion, but to tell her his. There was nothing she could say but "I'm happy for you, dear. Call when you can" before nestling back between the warm sheets.

By noon the following day a lengthy email arrived, detailing David's travel plans. He'd be at the dinner table by the following Friday and could remain (fork in hand) until Sunday afternoon. Not that he wished to impose on his mother to cook all his childhood favorites, but just in case she was in the mood he assured her he'd arrive with a good appetite.

Alex was amused and flattered. David had always had a way of charming her—or disarming her—to get exactly what he wanted. She immediately made out a menu for two dinners and a spectacular Sunday brunch. She also planned for an extra guest. This would be her perfect opportunity to introduce Charlie in a casual, familiar background where the two men could get acquainted and, hopefully, like each other. Until now David had bristled each time she spoke of her new relationship.

Whether it was that obstinate possessiveness a son feels about his mother or just flat-out jealousy, Alex didn't analyze. She remembered the friction surrounding Garrett; David had viewed another young man as competition. But this was different. Charlie was old enough to be David's father. Light-bulb moment: maybe that was it! Alex shook her head in disbelief. So many years had passed since the divorce; how could he still harbor resentment toward another man in his mother's life?

She shoved all this psychoanalyzing under the standing rib roast tucked in the market basket. As soon as Alex had overloaded the refrigerator with ingredients, she called Charlie. He had only a minute between classes: just long enough to commit to brunch.

"Honey, I can't make it for either dinner—I'm booked for both nights—but Sunday would be fine." Time enough for her two men to face each other with sunlight streaming through the windows and freshly made mimosas on the bar.

As anticipated, Alex's doorbell rang just before six o'clock on Friday. On the other side, ready to make his entrance, stood the son and the moon. David Silvers had come home, arms extended to full length to embrace every inch of his mother. The delicious aromas bursting from the kitchen only enhanced their exhilaration. Caught in the tailspin of being together, each spoke over the other, neither listening to what was being said, as the room seemed to swell with excitement. Two became a crowd, anxious to celebrate.

David did justice to his mother's efforts, consuming peanut butter chocolate chip pie (with his favorite cookie crumb crust) until he groaned contentedly, loosened his belt (as he'd seen older relatives do) to confirm approval, and sat back to watch his mother clear the table. As she loaded the dishwasher, Alex mentioned Sunday brunch—and their special guest. David didn't reply at first, but his reaction was evident. Even through the disruption of noisy silverware, David's sigh was a disappointment. Alex had hoped, perhaps unrealistically, that he'd be more receptive. She turned to see him staring straight at her, still not saying a word. He had gotten his point across with silence.

"David, darling, give Charlie a chance. He's really such a nice person, and he's important to me. Don't you trust my judgment?"

"Of course I do, Mom. But I see him differently. There's just something about him that makes me uneasy. He's a perpetual transient."

"But you've never even met him! It's not fair to be judgmental. You only know what little I've told you. Please keep an open mind."

Again, David didn't react. But it was obvious he was deep in concentration. Alex could almost see his thought process revolving.

Pushing back his chair, he rose from the table, shook his head with resignation, and declared himself too tired to continue the discussion. In the den he flipped on the TV and, after watching less than a program, fell asleep on the hide-a-bed. He later awoke, undressed to his underwear, and slept until midmorning.

The following afternoon slipped away too quickly, along with the money hidden in Alex's lingerie drawer—those coveted Ben Franklin bills she'd been saving for something special. Of course, she consoled herself, a weekend with her son was important enough to qualify for depletion. David needed to look his best for the interview. A new shirt and tie—and shoes, too—would give him the confidence to present himself well. It was good to relive the days when laughter came so easily. They teased and chattered and stopped for a latté, never once mentioning Charlie's name.

That evening David obliterated the food he hadn't consumed the night before. He then asked to borrow Alex's car to meet friends who still lived nearby. It was the same pitch from his youth: he gave his mother a quick kiss and an assurance he'd be careful, and advised her not to wait up.

"Just going out with the bros, Mom." And off David drove in search of, she was sure, someone who he'd never take home to mother.

Time alone allowed Alex to prepare the anticipated brunch. First she set the yeast dough for brioche. Then she set the table for the eggs benedict that would accompany the bread. Beautiful. The crystal stemware towered over gold-and-turquoise china. Polished flatware accented napkins cleverly folded into fans. A spray of silk flowers flowed from an ivory-colored vase, giving the table colors of the rainbow. All would be perfect. Everyone would get along.

By eleven the next morning David was still sleeping; even the delectable seduction of sizzling ham and fried potatoes with mushrooms and onions didn't tempt him awake. Twice Alex went in to check on him, finally resorting to tickling his arm to awaken her sleeping lion. David jolted up, asked the time, and was in the shower before Alex could measure the coffee. Not a moment too soon. Charlie used his key to let himself in. Alex looked up and there he was, smiling as he handed her a bottle of champagne.

"Oops, I forgot the orange juice for mimosas. Well, we'll just have to drink it straight," he teased.

"I have orange juice. I'll get the flutes out." Charlie shrugged, convinced they were about to dilute a good Brut.

At that point David entered the kitchen. He was now dressed neatly, hair newly washed and slicked down, but otherwise ready for the day. Before Alex could even begin introductions the two men extended their hands in a cordial greeting. Although David was inches taller, they looked straight at each other, eager to begin a dialogue. Alex deliberately left them alone, relieved to have food to prepare. There wasn't a better common denominator than sharing a meal.

The conversation was as active as their appetites. David told Charlie about his career aspirations, and Charlie spoke of his life on the road, with anecdotes about well-known musicians he had worked with. Alex didn't even have to speak. All she wanted to do was sit there, content.

After a while, David asked Charlie if he would play something, anything. Charlie was too flattered to refuse. They walked over to the rented keyboard, which fit snugly in the alcove off the hallway, almost as if the architect had designed it deliberately. Charlie paused for a moment and then began playing one of his favorites, a standard he was confident David would like: "Fly Me to the Moon." In a husky voice he half sang, half spoke the lyrics "and let me play among the stars."

David observed his mother gazing at Charlie and in an instant saw the lines of her face soften. Her eyes could see only him. It barely took a flash to realize why she desired this man, captivated by the majesty of his music, caught in the charm of his aura. Charlie was too absorbed in the pleasure of each note as it floated into the next to notice anything. David had what he'd wanted: the answer to his mother's involvement with someone so paradoxical to who she was and had always aspired to be.

He looked at his watch and exclaimed that the plane wouldn't wait for him, then excused himself to finish packing, Moments later he reappeared, baggage in hand, to say he'd already called a taxi. Alex looked disappointed, insisting she could drive him to the airport, but he was just as adamant in refusing the offer.

"No, Mom, you stay here and relax. This is easier." By the time he'd finished his sentence, a horn indicated his ride was waiting outside. With a quick handshake for Charlie and a lingering hug for his mother, David walked out the door, glancing back once to see Charlie again seated at the piano and Alex standing close in, her hand resting on his shoulder. The duffel he was holding suddenly felt one hundred pounds heavier.

It was two days before Alex got the call from Los Angeles. David apologized, insisting that he'd been busy interviewing, first with the office manager and then with the anticipated chief financial officer. Apparently he'd presented well and, after an introduction by his father, was hired to be the assistant to the assistant in the accounting department with the anticipation of advancement as earned. Alex, of course, was delighted for him—even to the extent of considering calling her former husband to congratulate him on their son's achievement. She did not.

David sounded frenzied with so much to do before the following Monday morning. Alex was anxious to hear his reaction to Charlie but knew it would have to wait until he'd found a place to live, a car to lease, and a bank in which to deposit his first paycheck.

Apparently David was just as eager to talk, for he called back the next evening. Before Alex could even ask, before she could say she'd thought the brunch went well, David monopolized the conversation. "Mom even with all this happening here, I can't stop thinking about you and Charlie—him at the piano, you gazing at him like he was some sort of genius. It's that music thing that fascinates you. If he sold insurance you wouldn't want him!"

"If he sold insurance he wouldn't be who he is! Give me some credit, David. Yes, I enjoy being in a room filled with wonderful music. But besides his talent, Charlie is really special: a good hearted friend—and fun, too."

"Charlie is all about Charlie, Mom. Just listen to his conversation. I don't know why you can't see it. Maybe this 'gift' he's got—and I will give him that, he's awesome—has made him feel entitled to have whoever he wants or pleases him at the moment."

"You're reading him all wrong, David."

But before Alex could object any further, David ranted on, "Did you ever figure out why he wants you, Mom? What he gets out of your relationship? You represent all that he isn't. You supply the propriety, the stability he lacks. To be crude about it, Mother, you're a class act and he wants the package."

"David, please believe me. My eyes are wide open, and I do see reality. I know you can't understand this, but being with Charlie makes me happy. However long it may last, I'll be with him."

"For God's sake, Mother, you sound like some lyric to a song. But that ends too! I give up. Go be with him. I've got my own life to worry about."

There was nothing left to say; each held to their own point of view, convinced it was the right one. Alex remained quiet. Her tears made no sound as David growled an abrupt goodbye.

10

A CHANCE TO DANCE

Days were routine and life predictable. To many people this would be welcome: comfortable, safe. But to Charlie Coleman and his Gypsy soul, continuity edged on boredom. He'd taught at Northridge nearly five years—long enough to have a solid reputation. But in his entire career he had never remained at the same job in the same place for so long, and the jagged edges were starting to fray.

Usually good-natured, he became impatient with details. His easy laugh became less frequent, replaced by only a flash of smile. Alex worried it was something she was doing, should be doing, because it was affecting her, too. So, on a particular Sunday when he hadn't played into the early hours, she invited him over for brunch.

After softening his disposition with a three-cheese omelet and warm lemon raspberry muffins, she began a gentle questioning, wary of venturing too far and provoking his temper.

"Charlie, darling, I've sensed your uneasiness lately. Is there anything I can do to help?"

Charlie pretended to sip his coffee, but they both knew it was only a stall. There was some subject out there too difficult to put into words. Finally, the cup was empty. His alibi swallowed.

"Matter of fact, Allie, I've been wanting to talk to you about something. I suppose this is as good a time as ..." His voice trailed off as he leaned toward her, lightly tapping her hand with his fingertips as if he was beginning a melody.

"You know, I've been here at school several years."

Alex sat straight up, anticipating negative news.

"And much as I've tried, I just can't get my head around staying in one place too long. It's just not in me."

Alex could only respond, "Yes, yes go on. I'm listening."

"Well, you know I'm tight with my musician friends, and we all know what's going on in the profession. Word got out that Jake Stone—you've probably heard of him, that writer-director for public television—is planning a series about twentieth-century musicians, legends of our time. He wants to do it soon." He shook his head. "There aren't many left." He continued, "So I heard he'd been looking for guys like me, who've been around a long time, to do an in-depth study of their career—kind of live their life, tell their story and what they've contributed, so younger generations can appreciate their musical heritage. It'll be a five-or-six-part documentary on national television with plenty of funding—a really big deal. So it's like this: I called Jake's office a couple of weeks ago to say I was interested in his project. I didn't even think he'd call me back. But a couple of days later he did. He actually knew who I was, heard my work, what I've done. I've got to admit, I was flattered."

Alex sat very still, waiting to hear the final crescendo.

"Not a week after that I got a second call. We had a long conversation. It went well. By this time I knew I was in the top few. But there were other guys too—all talented—so I hung up the phone and tried to forget about it. Four days ago the call came through." Charlie sat forward, peering into Alex's eyes to accentuate his excitement.

"Jake asked me to go to New Orleans for as long as it takes —maybe a year—to create an 'as he lives it' study of—and get this, Allie—Pete Procter!"

Alex nearly gasped. Even she was aware of the renowned clarinetist. "Pete Procter!" was all she could sputter out.

Charlie had to laugh. He hadn't expected such a reaction.

"This is the deal: I stalled Jake for a few days, telling him I'd have to clear it with the college. But to be honest, I'd already talked with the dean. He's allowing me a sabbatical; there's enough staff to cover my classes. Meanwhile, I'll get all my living expenses paid, plus I figured when I'm not with Pete, I can play gigs on my own. Allie, honey, I'm free to go! But I don't want to leave you here. Come with me. I need you with me!"

The entire English language vanished from her mind. Not a single word, not even a syllable resembling a word, occurred to her. Alex was absolutely dumbfounded. All she could do was stare at Charlie in disbelief for several minutes. He began to chuckle with amusement at the astonishment on her face.

"Well, say something. You can't just sit there and stare at me. I'm not that pretty!"

At that, the two began to laugh together, first from sheer shock, and then with a burst of anticipation.

"Charlie Coleman, I can't believe what you've been up to! You want me to go with on this expedition? You must be crazy —and maybe I'm crazy, too. It sounds fabulous, but how can I go? I've got classes, responsibilities. How can I just leave Dr. Benneton? He's been so kind to me, so helpful."

"Tell him you've enraptured with a lunatic musician and you must follow him to the ends of the earth."

"Louisiana isn't the ends of the earth, Charlie."

"But it's the end of the rainbow for us, baby. That pot of gold is waiting—and so are the deep-fried beignets! Tell me you'll come, honey. I won't be happy without you."

"Charlie, you'd be happy anywhere there's eight-eight keys

on a board. As long as there's a note to be played. I will tell you I'll think about it. Now, let me clear these dishes. I've got assignments to work on."

Charlie sensed he couldn't push her any further. He rose from the table, grabbed Alex around the waist and danced her to the door, singing in his best baritone, "When the Saints Go Marchin' In."

Alex looked at him, still stunned. Still smiling.

LIKE ALL PROBLEMS in search of a solution, this one had to be confronted—if Alex was ever to get off antacids. Between classes one morning, before she could give herself an excuse, Alex phoned Dean Benneton. Amelia put her call right through; he was available to talk. Somehow, when she heard his voice, she momentarily lost hers. "Alex, is that you? Are you all right, my dear? I can hardly hear you."

"Yes, yes, Dean. It must be my allergies today. Could I come in to talk? There's something on my mind."

"Certainly. How about tomorrow, late afternoon, when you're through for the day?"

"Thanks, I'll be there."

The following twenty-four hours were unsettling. Alex rehearsed opening statements, selling points, and concluding decisions. She alternated pragmatism and emotional appeals. But nothing she was prepared to say would match what she was going to hear.

The hallway was cast in gloom as day evolved into darkness. Amelia had, apparently left early, leaving the door to the dean's office slightly ajar. When Alex entered, she felt an unfamiliar emptiness. A voice called out as her footsteps made rhythmic clicks on the hardwood floor.

"Come in, Alex. I'm glad to see you." Dr. Benneton's warm greeting helped to erase Alex's anxiety. His massive desk was in its usual state of organized disarray; the papers were piled in small heaps he alone could decipher. It was a world with only one occupant. Pity the frustrated cleaning staff who would dare to straighten his strategy. The dean himself looked tired. Working so hard at his age was beginning to show, even in his eyes, as he frequently removed his glasses to massage around them.

"What can I do for you, Alex? What's the problem?"

Alex didn't dare hesitate or even move in her chair, secretly fearing she'd leap up and run out of the room to safety.

"Charlie Coleman asked me to go to New Orleans with him. He's taking a leave of absence to do research on a documentary for public TV." Alex continued with details as the dean listened intently. Finally—and mercifully—she finished delivering all the necessary information and paused to breathe.

Dr. Benneton stared down at his desk, seemingly interested in the papers before him, though it was obvious he was not reading. When he did look up, his eyes bored into Alex.

"So, what do you want to do? What do you want to hear me say? Obviously, you're thinking seriously about joining him, or you would have refused the offer and not come to me for approval. It's that simple."

Alex nodded. By this point she had forgotten her well-rehearsed comments and could only express her feelings.

"Oh Dr. Benneton, I know what you must be thinking—how could a woman of my years with good sense do something so disruptive? There are ten reasons why I shouldn't go and only one to explain why I should."

"And what's that?"

"Because I want to be with Charlie. He charms me with his laughter. He reaches into who I am—all I can be—and makes me feel the sun has captured me in its warmth."

"That's more than one reason, Alex." They both paused to savor the moment's humor.

The dean continued, "I can't tell you what to do, Alex. I know that's why you came here: to give me the responsibility of telling you not to go or, conversely, saying you should. But I can't do that. It's your decision alone. I can tell you I will have to hire your replacement. Much as I'd like to keep the position open, your department is too small and I have a school to run. You've been an excellent asset here, but if you leave us now I can't guarantee I can reinstate you even though I would very much like to. You're forfeiting future security. Think what that will mean years from now."

There was a strained silence between them. Dr. Benneton began again. "Conversely, I do understand more than you think. Be greedy with life, my friend. Grab with both hands all it has to offer. It has a way of flying away, and if you're very lucky you'll get a chance to bask in that golden sun you spoke of. Ultimately, you'll do what you want to do. Whatever you decide, Alex, I wish you the best."

With that the dean pulled himself up from his desk chair in a not-too-subtle signal that the discussion was over.

ALEX FELT MORE uneasiness than ever, and it was only to increase. There was another person whose opinion greatly mattered. Later that same evening, when calm had replaced the stress of the day, she put in a call to David. It was late, but he was a night person.

"Hello, darling, it's your mom."

"I could tell that," he replied with amusement. "What's up? You never call this late. Is everything okay?"

"Well, yes and no." Alex nearly sputtered the next sentences, gaining momentum from sheer nerves. She poured out as much as she could as fast as she could, afraid to pause, fearful she couldn't continue. When she finally concluded,

Alex stopped abruptly, anticipating David's thunderous reaction from the West Coast.

Instead he remained detached, responding in a controlled voice.

"Mom, I'm sure you've considered your choices. You're too sensible, too grounded not to have thought this through. But you can't just throw this at me. I need to think about it, too. Give me some time. Right now I've got to get back to my reading."

"Oh, David, I've been alone so long. This could be my last chance. Don't you understand what I'm going through?" Alex heard herself trying too hard. Before her son could end the conversation, she blurted out a final plea—the strained emotion in her voice pleading for acceptance.

"What do you want me to say, Mom? You throw this crazy idea at me. How did you think I'd take it?" David's articulation became more emphatic, biting at each syllable to emphasize his point.

Alex realized it would only escalate, so she wished him a hasty goodbye and they both hung up. Each faced a night filled with anger at both the looming problem and, momentarily, each other.

Alex might well have slept in the subway for all the rest she got. Finally dozing off, she awakened so early that even the birds hadn't sung their serenade. The coffee tasted bitter; the toast was dry as cardboard. It was no use pretending the day ahead would be productive. The only relief she felt was standing under the spray of a warm shower, allowing the droplets to moisturize her skin and the humid vapors to circulate as they swirled around her. She would put herself on automatic pilot today, mindlessly relying on a proven routine. Her assistants could cover for her.

Tonight she would call David again—and listen thoughtfully to him. At least they would quell their tempers. She would catch him earlier, soon after dinner, when he felt a surge of energy. Just as she entered the condo's elevator, Alex heard her purse start ringing. Two neighbors smiled while a third person pretended to ignore the intrusion. Luckily her floor was next, and she quickly unlocked her door before reaching to retrieve her phone. It was David. Obviously he'd had as restless a day and needed to smooth out the previous night's turmoil.

"Hi, Mom, figured you'd be home about now." He sounded tired.

"Hello, dear. I was just about to call you. We need to resolve this conflict—if you want to call it that." Alex paused before continuing, "David, I don't want you to feel I'm letting you down because I may change my lifestyle."

"Change! Mom, you're turning your life upside down! Do you realize what you're giving up to run off with Charlie?"

"I'm not running off! I am considering joining him for maybe a year. David, I'm burned out from being sensible—doing whatever I was supposed to do, what everyone else expected of me. There's a world full of excitement out there, and all I've ever done was view it from a damn kitchen window! Please, please allow me to dance on a silver moon."

The phone went silent. Alex didn't know if they'd lost their connection or David wasn't speaking to her. She held on, her fingers going numb around the cell. A sound began to emanate. A breathiness, like someone gasping deeply for air.

"David, are you all right? You're scaring me!"

"I'm okay, Mom. Just give me a minute. Better yet, I'll call you back." The connection abruptly ended.

Alex sensed what he was going through. She, too, needed to relax and breathe easier. Within minutes, David called again, this time sounding more controlled.

"Mom, listen: you do what you want. It doesn't really matter what I think. You're going to go if you want to—and it sounds like you've got your mind set already. You don't need me to justify your life."

"But David, do you see this from my point of view?"

"No, Mom, I don't. I only see what you're losing—a good job, future security. I'm an accountant. Two and two always have to make four. You're shorting yourself and settling for three and a half."

"David, it's not the end of the world. I'll come back."

"Back to what, Mom? To starting all over again finding work at your age? How the hell are you going to get along? I'm just beginning my career; I can't support you!"

"I've thought it through carefully. First, I'll sublet my condo while I'm away. That will bring in a monthly check. Then I'll have you convert those stocks from the divorce settlement into an annuity. Next, I'll talk to Dr. Benneton. I'm sure he'd hire me back if he could."

"*If he could*. That's the key phrase here, Mom. Get real: we both know your position will be filled right off. There's not going to be an opening waiting for you. Your career at Northridge is history; and don't tell me you'll start teaching somewhere. You're always saying how your back hurts. So tell me, how are you going to live? Or are you just resigned to being Charlie's woman?"

David's voice intensified with each sentence, growing so loud Alex had to extend her arm away to soften the amplification.

"We've always been so close. I just assumed you'd understand. Your life is sprawling ahead. Mine is mostly in the rearview mirror, and I've opened too many doors to nothing. To going home each night to make one piece of chicken, one baked potato. David, darling, I need to be free to dance before it's too late."

"Are you in love with him?"

Alex thought hard before she replied. She owed her son—and herself—the truth. "No, David, I'm not *in* love, but I do love him. I'm acutely aware there's a difference. Charlie and I are close friends. We have a special relationship, and that's enough." She drew a deep breath before continuing. "Charlie could have had someone half my age, far more attractive, but he wants *me* with him."

David's voice edged with emotion. "Mother, look at yourself in the mirror. You're a great-looking woman. But more than that, when you walk in the room it's obvious how sharp you are. Give yourself more credit. Everyone sees this—Charlie included—why can't you?"

Alex struggled to reply. "You're getting too upset, too reactive. Don't worry about me. I promise I'll have all these details worked out. David, David are you there?"

"Yes, I'm here, Mom. I don't want to talk about this any more. You do what you want. You don't listen anyway."

The discussion was terminated. David was correct when he predicted that with all the advice and sound logic offered, his mother would ultimately do what she wanted. He didn't know, however, there was one person who could change her mind: Ted Hudson. Reticent to admit it to herself, Alex thought that if he objected to her being with Charlie, she'd cancel out. All he had to do was say life had been empty without her and there was a chance they could reunite again. It was a long shot but worth trying.

What time was it in Boca? Where would he be, and, more to the point, would he be alone? Maybe she should wait until tomorrow. Play it safe. But there was no such zone as "safe" with Ted. She stared at the numerals on the phone for a moment, then pressed the appropriate sequence. Two rings later, a familiar voice replied, "Well, if it isn't my beautiful Alexandra."

After a cordial chat about her classes and his golf, Alex began an explanation for her call. Ted interrupted abruptly, "Why are you telling me this, Alex? You're free to go with this guy. I'm not going to stop you. I can't. We've been all over this.

You knew my situation then, and it hasn't changed. Go down there, have all the fun you can in the Big Easy. It's a great city! Listen, Beautiful, it's late and I've got an early tee-off tomorrow. All the best, Alex. Good to hear from you." There was a pause. Alex had nearly hung up when she heard Ted speak again— this time in a hushed tone, so counter to his previous bravado. "I'm sorry, Alex, I'm sorry I can't give you what you want. What I want too, honey. I wish things could be ..." He faltered midsentence before ending the call.

Alex sat very still, angry with herself for exposing her vulnerability. What had she fantasized? Ted had a predictable response: defensive, impatient. Yet there was that whisper of tenderness suggesting that he, too, was trapped in a chasm of regret.

The time of contemplation was over. The decision made, Alexandra would accompany her Charlie to New Orleans. Although on the surface it appeared to be irresponsible—actually impetuous to most colleagues—she stood by her commitment, ignoring the stares of disbelief and hurtful comments. Reassuring herself that others were probably envious of her adventurous spirit, she consoled herself that it was all right to disrupt the tidy world she'd always clung to.

Charlie, of course, was elated. Within the week he had located a small house to rent in the French Quarter. It was right on Conti Street, adjacent to the club owned by the icon Pete Procter (and thus convenient for him to sit in when another musician canceled). Though the home was modest (no space for houseguests), he assured Alex she'd love lounging on the balcony. The online picture showed a yellow clapboard exterior enhanced with elaborate grillwork. Four wire baskets filled with brightly colored flowers and greenery swung freely from the porch ceiling, giving the façade the look of a perpetual party: Come, join the fun!

However, there was much to do before departure. Alex had

given Dr. Benneton her promise to complete the curriculum for the next three months. That way, he felt, it would be easier for her replacement to acquaint himself (yes, she was to be replaced by a young chef lured away from a local restaurant) with procedures before improvising on his own. That translated into many late nights and weekends of accumulating information, developing innovative menus and testing each several times.

Renting out her condo was the easy part. Amelia had a friend who had a friend who'd recently transferred to the city. Assured that the young woman was of good character, Alex asked for and received more than a fair fee, guaranteed the first of each month.

David remained stubbornly David. Adamantly opposed to his mother's new choice of lifestyle, he loved her too much to stay angry. The evening before her departure he actually called to wish her good luck. He did, however, decline the standing invitation to visit, insisting that he didn't want to sleep on the living room sofa.

Charlie decided it would be best if he went out a week ahead; that would give him time to open the house, make any essential improvements, and meet Pete Procter. He called Alex about seven each night—right before leaving for the club for a rambunctious session of blaring horns. He nearly came through the phone with exuberance. Their house was ready, the weather was warm, and he couldn't wait for her plane to land.

11

SOUTHERN COMFORT

During the flight down, Alex stared out the window, replaying the final moments as she closed the door on the condo and on her life as it had been. She could not signal the airline attendant to tell the pilot to turn around. Her journey to the silver moon had begun.

Charlie was to meet her at the statue of Louis Armstrong in the center of the terminal. He was late. Burdened with a cart overflowing with a multitude of baggage, she peered in each direction, anxious for his arrival. The plane had been right on schedule, which she assumed he knew. From somewhere near the exit the sounds of a trombone coasted through cavernous corridors, a welcome to the city personified by the music it was famous for. It helped put her at ease.

Suddenly she felt two hands boldly grabbing at her backside. Startled, she swung around to see Charlie's broad smile as his eyes twinkled with delight.

"Sorry I'm late. I stopped to talk with a few guys in that group over there." He nodded in the direction of the trombonist. "Friendly city. I've already made contacts. C'mon, honey, let's get out of here."

Alex grabbed her carry-on and followed Charlie as he struggled with most, if not all, of her wardrobe. The house was just as she'd pictured, only more charming. Obviously quite old, and built long and narrow in the traditional shotgun style, it fortunately had a renovated kitchen. Charlie had bought fresh flowers for every room and scrawled "Welcome Alexandra!" on a large cardboard sign, which he propped in front of the brick fireplace. He'd even gone to the grocery store and filled the refrigerator with blue shell crab, rice with tomatoes and sweet bell peppers, and a plastic container filled with some sort of liquid resembling soup. A large grouping of bananas sat on the kitchen table—Charlie's interpretation of a centerpiece. It was all so thoughtful, almost overwhelming. The couple sat down for their premier meal in the home they shared, confident they'd made the right decision. Promptly at eight that evening, Charlie kissed Alex goodnight and left for the club, leaving her alone on her first night in NOLA.

Pete Proctor—the music "doctor"—began the first set at nine. Charlie had been playing keyboard with the group since he'd arrived. It gave him an intimate view of Pete at work or play. It was also good money. Alex couldn't object. At first she was glad to have time for her own projects: delving through magazines, getting ideas on how to accessorize the rooms. During the day she'd shop for towels and tableware and an attractive bedspread, though the latter was rarely used because of their opposite sleep schedules. But it was okay. They were settling in and getting comfortable, both with their lifestyle and with each other.

Charlie was easy to get along with in New Orleans. No artistic moods or temperament. Although Alex wished he'd be home more, the joyfulness of his presence surrounded her; she'd walk into the bedroom and find bouquets of fresh flowers. Sometimes he'd sneak over to Café Du Monde to indulge her with powdered-sugar beignets. Unexpectedly, he'd embrace her, then whirl her around and conclude with a lingering kiss. He told her she was wonderful. He made her laugh when she seemed lonely and consoled her by playing tender ballads whenever she spoke of missing David. He held her tightly, making all regrets disappear.

Charlie had never eaten so well. Whatever Alex served him was declared "Delicious!" Creole and Cajun food had not been in her repertoire, but she began exploring (and adoring) this new style of cooking combined with classic French cuisine.

There came a time, however, when the interior decorating was complete and the sweet touches weren't enough. Charlie's eight o'clock kiss became the prelude to an evening spent mindlessly watching television just to hear the voice of others in the room. This silence was reminiscent of too many years spent alone. Storm clouds were gathering and the darkness that loomed overhead was ominous.

One Sunday afternoon, when Charlie hadn't had a booking at a hotel brunch, Alex told him to sit in a chair and listen. He seemed surprised after she expressed her concern, insisting he hadn't realized her frustration.

"Allie, I'm so sorry you've felt neglected. When you got here you seemed so content to stay home. But I can fix that, honey. It's my job to be around Pete. When he included me in the band, I couldn't refuse. Musicians are a tight group. Word gets around, and when other gigs came up I just naturally accepted. I guess I was too flattered to say no. So why don't you start coming with me? You'll love it as much as I do. Please, baby!"

Alex stared at him for a long moment, watching as he sat there, a copy of *Downbeat* tucked beside him. David had been right. It was all about Charlie. Compromise was not an option when it came to his music.

"Stay home sometime. Spend the evening with me."

"I can't, Alex. Don't ask me to. You know I can't. You come with me."

Game over. The contender conceded.

Pete's club looked more like a cave. Although she entered with Charlie through the stage door, Alex could see a lengthy line of customers in front, clamoring to be admitted. Waves of laughter and chatter flowed from those willing to exchange their wages for a raucous few hours. The crowd congregated beneath the radiance of a garish neon marquee that promised all who entered would experience an evening of musical history. The sign advertised "Pete Proctor the Music Doctor" with a caricature figure wearing a white medical jacket as he grasped his clarinet with obvious pleasure.

As Alex entered the main room she immediately noticed an enormous reproduction of the marquee hanging over the massive bar. Other than that the décor was beyond simple. Charlie later explained it was deliberate, keeping the focus on the stage.

The walls were dark, and the wood tables and chairs were placed so closely together one needed to squeeze sideways to wiggle in. Plastic bowls filled with salted peanuts were centered on each table in hopes of encouraging thirst.

As expected, the far end of the room was filled with instruments. Charlie's piano, to the left of the horns and percussion, stood ready for the night's action. Guests began filling in, seating themselves as quickly as they could maneuver through. Within minutes the musicians came on stage, taking their respective places. The drummer, sticks already in hand, waited to introduce a rhythmic beat. Charlie ambled on last. He peered over the row of lighting to search for Alex in the audience. She blew him a kiss; he smiled in response and then sat down to lure the audience from everyday reality to a place where dreams come true. With every woman gazing in admiration, Alex delighted knowing it was only she who Charlie would come home to; only her body he desired in the night.

The music seemed to emanate from their souls, each note a

tribute to the exuberance of life. Whatever problems tomorrow would bring dissolved into the exhilaration of the moment.

The hours flew, and before she realized it the band began "When it's Sleepy Time Down South"—their signature encore —and the patrons begrudgingly dispersed. Alex glanced at her watch and for a split second thought the battery had stopped. Up later than she had been since college, she turned to hear Pete thanking everyone for coming and reminding them to drive home carefully. Two minutes later Charlie was standing beside her asking, "What did you think?" But before Alex could answer he continued, "C'mon, let's go grab some breakfast, hon."

Alex's impulse was to blurt out, "Are you crazy!" but the last time she'd eaten was technically yesterday and the thought of chicken and waffles was tempting. The all-night grill was close by. There wasn't one empty table; apparently it was the favorite destination of those who welcomed dawn. Pete didn't join them, but several of the others did, critiquing their recent performance to the final note.

Slivers of daylight streaked across receding darkness. Alex yawned impolitely, and Charlie got the message: it was time to go home. Alex could hardly splash water on her face before diving into bed. Conversely, Charlie said he was too stimulated to sleep and preferred to read for a while. A creature of the night, he was conditioned to those hours.

For the next weeks Alex tried her best to adjust. But being nocturnal was different after a lifetime of opposite hours. Her energy siphoned away and her stomach felt uncomfortable eating at such odd hours. She suggested an obvious solution: during a break, Charlie could escort her home. It was a quick walk that allowed him enough time to return to the club before the next set. But he disagreed, insisting those twenty-plus minutes were used to review new charts and make changes in the program. Alex knew the truth, recalling how often she'd seen the men standing by the back door enjoying a drink and smoking their hand-rolled cigarettes. It was, however, nonnegotiable. She didn't dare walk the dark streets of the French Quarter alone. She would have to yield to his bizarre schedule.

Eventually Alex adjusted to sleeping during much of the day and staying awake most of the night. It never felt right, but in order to spend time with Charlie, she acquiesced.

Communicating with David was another challenge. Being in the Pacific time zone meant he was working when his mother slept, and she couldn't call from the club when he was available. Sundays seemed their best chance to talk. Alex would burst into conversation about the week's activities: how the fans at Pete's Place applauded Charlie's solos, and her recent acquisitions for their quaint yellow house in the Quarter. David seemed to listen. At least he remained silent and didn't yawn. When she had finished with all the flowery descriptions, he would simply reply, "That's great, Mom," and then change the subject.

He, too, was experiencing some success. Although it was stressful for him to learn the regulations and procedures, his manager appreciated the long hours he'd been putting in. In fact, that was about all he'd been doing. His only enjoyment was going to the nearby library to get something to read besides tax forms. This was not her David. Alex knew the metamorphosis wouldn't last long. He'd soon find friends to join him for a beer, and his well-tuned antenna would eventually locate a pretty admirer.

The suggestion of a visit was never mentioned. Alex assumed he'd reject her invitation, using his work as a perfect excuse for the truth. David had no intention of encouraging—or participating—in his mother's current lifestyle. Politely tolerant was his limit; Alex could expect no more. They left it at that: agreeing to disagree, each wishing the other the best of tomorrows.

When Charlie wasn't performing or sleeping or working on a new arrangement, he was on the computer, recreating his impression of Pete Proctor and the environment in which he thrived. Long drafts were sent to Jake, who in turn adapted the information for the television series. Often Alex was asked for her opinion as Charlie read her the copy. As creative as he was, English composition wasn't his expertise.

"Calm down, Charlie. You shouldn't have taken the job if it does this to you!" She chided over a particularly frustrating page.

"Dammit, Alex, I didn't know it'd be this hard!"

"Well, it is, and we'll just have to plow through it. Go play your piano. I'll try to rewrite that paragraph. And the next one, too."

So it went, with Charlie depending more and more on Alex's experience explaining cooking. Never had she imagined that converting culinary techniques would enable her to describe a clarinetist. Jake responded often, encouraging Charlie to delve more intensely into the Legend and His Times. What had begun as a temporary project became a surging whirlpool drawing him in too deeply to escape. He could not, would not leave Alex behind. She was his partner in this upside-down world of crazy hours, free-spirited friends, and the uninhibited life of those whose sole priority was enjoying themselves in the responses they received from others. The applause was the breath they inhaled. Unconventional and spontaneous, it was paradoxical to all she had ever known.

A network of musicians—all of whom seemed to know of each other—met many afternoons. Charlie was an integral part of this group. He asked Alex often to accompany him to the Marigny district, where, in a bar on Frenchmen Street, he'd meet with his friends and buy them drinks in exchange for their stories about jazz greats. Alex did go along occasionally, but she felt uncomfortable. She wasn't a member of this exclusive society, and their conversation eluded her. Besides, it seemed wasteful to drink the afternoon away; she'd find something better to do. As thrilling as it was to witness daybreak looming across the defiant onyx sky, her lifetime of nine-to-five was calling her back. She realized the need to retreat to a healthier routine. She also realized she and Charlie should have a talk. Soon.

Before Charlie could make plans for Sunday afternoon, Alex suggested they stroll down to the river. Although it was quite warm, the humidity wasn't bothersome, and she insisted the exercise would do them both good. Charlie seemed surprised. The only calisthenics he ever did was flexing his fingers around a glass. They walked as far as the first bench available.

"So why are we here, baby? What's going on with you?"

Alex could read into Charlie's intonation. He knew what she was thinking before she'd even answered.

"Charlie, you're a love, and I'm fascinated with this city but ..."

"Get to the problem, Allie. You're not happy."

"Oh, yes I am! You always jump to the negative. I am happy here. It's just that," she paused briefly, then blurted out, "I need more to do. I can't go through my life piggybacking on yours, the way you spend each day—or should I say, night. It's not who I've always been. Charlie, I need to do something for myself."

"What, for instance?"

"Well, I've been investigating all this Southern cuisine. I thought I could possibly get a part-time job, maybe at a barbeque place or even just making po'boy sandwiches somewhere in the neighborhood. It would be a new experience I'd enjoy."

"You can't be serious, Alex! You work days and me work

nights? When the hell would we see each other? I want you with me."

"Don't get so upset, Charlie. It was only an idea. I'll think about it some more. But do understand, I need to have something for myself."

His reaction was unexpected.

"Listen hard, Alexandra. Life doesn't come with a dress rehearsal. This is it, baby. For you and me both."

"I know, Charlie. C'mon, let's get a chicory coffee. Say you understand."

"Okay, I understand." He reached over to touch the ticklish spot on the back of her neck, forcing Alex to laugh with him. The discussion was closed. Or so he thought.

Mardi Gras came with all its tumultuous exuberance. Charlie was booked every day, sometimes playing back-to-back events. He arrived home too exhausted to eat, preferring to flop on the bed fully dressed. Alex would remove his shoes, cover him with a cotton blanket, and count the days until Lent.

Finally, the festivities were over. Being on her own the previous week had allowed her time to explore possibilities. It was imperative that she have a concise plan to present to Charlie. Knowing him, it was the only way he'd agree.

For many months, on her frequent visits to the nearby French Market, Alex had stopped at a little spot called Sweet Sally's. It was not much larger than the long counter with six or eight stools its canopy shaded. In the back she could see ovens and a worktable. The sign overhead read "Rum Custards, Mocha Soufflés, and Banana Bread Pudding—The Best in New Orleans!" An irresistible aroma of buttery sweetness drifted outwards, defying anyone to contradict its pledge of excellence.

Miss Sally herself looked to be one hundred years old—and she'd been baking desserts for every one of them. She was a little lady, with wisps of white hair tumbling capriciously from her pink-sequined cap over a face blushed from the heat of the ovens. Despite her advanced age, she moved with agility, sliding one tray after another into the oven's heated interior. With a rhythm all their own, her hands manipulated each confection with a deftness and confidence achieved only by decades of experience.

Alex knew she would ask Sally for a job. It felt right. With her extensive résumé in hand, she watched until the customer line dwindled, then approached the counter girl to inquire if Sally would see her. Within minutes she was told to go back around.

"I'll be with you as soon as I pull these pans out." Sally's voice was as small as its owner. Wiping her face with a moistened towel, Sally approached a few minutes later with what appeared to be a smile. It was disconcerting, however, because as her cheeks inflated her mouth opened to reveal a conspicuous gap between her teeth, resulting in a rather odd but pleasant expression that Alex interpreted as a positive sign.

"I've admired your, ah, shop here, and wanted to know if you needed some part-time help. Here are my qualifications." As Alex extended the papers, Sally paused to clean the steam from her glasses on the hem of her well-stained apron. She glanced quickly, not taking time to evaluate each sentence.

"You're hired. Hours are nine to two. Can't pay much more than minimum, but all you can eat while you're here. Start tomorrow, Alexandra. Oh, and welcome to Sweet Sally's!"

Alex was flabbergasted. With all her experience and many accomplishments, she had never been accepted with such confidence. Now all she had to do was go home and convince Charlie.

She walked slowly, as if she could put off the argument that was certain to erupt. Each step brought her closer to the unavoidable. Charlie was still home when she opened the door. Ironically, he had decided to work on new arrangements.

"Where have you been, baby? I got up and you weren't here."

"Sorry, Charlie, I thought you'd be out playing someplace. I was over at the French Market. You know how I enjoy visiting all those food stands."

"So did you buy anything? Something good? I haven't eaten yet today. I was waiting for you."

Alex peered straight at him and blurted out what she needed to say: "I got a job, Charlie, helping a nice little lady make desserts."

"You what? Alex, you must be joking! Why would you do that? I take all these gigs to make money for us—for you!"

Alex shook her head in frustration. "Charlie, be honest with yourself—and with me! You play all the time because it keeps you alive. It's oxygen to you. Without music you wouldn't be able to breathe. I understand that, but let's be real here. It's not about money. I need to feel that same high as you, that same intoxication with life. I can't continue spending every day and night following you around. Surely you can see where this is leading. I need to feel useful."

"But you are useful. Here, with me."

"Oh, Charlie, you're just being obstinate. Your ego's in the way. You know damn well what I'm talking about, how I'm feeling. I've got to do something with who I am. I owe myself that. Don't look so wounded. It's only part-time. I'll be home before you even wake up. You won't be inconvenienced at all."

Charlie chose not to reply. He turned back to the piano as if to imply there was nothing left to add. They both knew that in the final analysis, Alexandra would do as she wished.

12

BLUES IN THE NIGHT

After the confrontation they settled into a compromising routine. Alex raced home at two o'clock every afternoon to make sure Charlie would eat a sensible meal. She knew it would be the only healthy nutrition he'd consume that day. His usual break-of-dawn menu of Deep-Fried Everything continued, along with consuming whatever the bartender happened to be pouring as he approached.

Although Jake Stone kept in touch, the project was slow to develop. There were so many details, many of which became problems the executive staff couldn't agree upon. Charlie (with Alex's help) sent in what he considered to be interesting interviews and insights about an original American art form. It often tried his patience; he was not accustomed to being edited or enduring the microscopic scrutiny of directors and producers. Often he'd turn to Alex to tell her to finish the correspondence.

"What the hell difference does it make! They're gonna chop it apart anyway!" he'd growl with disgust. But so long as those checks kept coming, he continued to collect unique sound bites of history. There was no apparent deadline, as the series premiere had been extended indefinitely in search of new sponsors. That suited Charlie just fine. He was satisfied to have each week mirror the last: an evening performance followed by an after-hours session with any musicians who happened by, and then a fast meal and home to sleep half the day away. He often met with friends to have a drink (under the guise of research) before having dinner with Alex and repeating the night's routine. A perfect schedule, to his thinking.

For a while Alex agreed. Her days were free to pursue a new opportunity. Sweet Sally's was a conglomeration of customers. It was continuous fun to watch their faces light up as they tasted their first bite of dessert. Some actually uttered moaning sounds, while others attempted to grin approval as they chewed. All were effusive with compliments. Sweet Sally, her head down as she prepared the next order, would murmur a thank-you, never allowing the customer to see her smile. Self-conscious about her appearance, she seemed more comfortable retreating to the background to bake her scrumptious creations.

Whenever Alex could break away from the counter, she hovered over Sally while studying the expertise of masterful hands cajoling a cupful of flour to dance to her whim with an artistry never demonstrated in school, a finesse never to be forgotten. Alex knew that someday she, too, must emulate this gift.

By afternoon, after rushing to give Charlie his lunch, Alex needed to relax—but there was a never-ending stack of material waiting to send to Jake. Many times she'd barely finish before making dinner. That in itself was an adjustment. Their Northern menu of Yankee pot roast had been replaced by Southern cuisine. The delicacy of seafood, fresh from the Gulf waters, was easy to prepare after an active day. Charlie was an agreeable recipient—unaccustomed to any meal of quality after decades of burgers and fries.

By evening Alex was quite content to slip on a robe and watch a sitcom. But Charlie, eager for a night of cool company and hot music, often requested that she come along to wherever he was playing. Mostly it was Pete's Place. She'd beg off, insisting it was hard to get up for work the next morning, but there was something of an eight-year-old in Charlie. His head would droop down as though he was being punished. He wouldn't get outwardly angry or grumble anything in retaliation, but Alex could read his body language. Then she would acquiesce—if not out of guilt, then from flattery. If it meant that much to him to have her in the audience, she'd be there, applauding from her special table nearest the piano.

For a while it worked out. She'd stay as late as she could, then take a taxi home. But as months edged toward a year, Alex had to explain gently—and frequently—that it was becoming too difficult. Sweet Sally's had caught on with the tourists. Several hotel concierges had been suggesting the place, and business was going through the roof. (That is to say, it would have, had there been an actual roof on the booth instead of a canvas awning!) Charlie understood the logic and regretfully relented. The result was that he went out and she stayed in, each pursuing their own ambition. The course was inevitable: two people pulling from the center in diametrically opposite directions. In their determination to succeed on their own they were jeopardizing what they had once found: each other.

Neither would acknowledge the strain. Call it denial or plain stubbornness—surely they were too world-worn to have been naïve—but as time passed, the fabric of their relationship began to tear at the seams.

"Pete's thinking about opening on Sunday afternoons for a couple sets—catch all the brunch crowd. What do you think?"

"Well, that sounds like fun. If you do play, I'll tell Sally I'm available. She's always complaining she wants to stay at church to help with their charity lunch."

Their conversations became predictable; each anticipated where the other was going. It even infiltrated their lovemaking. Charlie would awaken Alex when he crawled into bed, just hours before her alarm rang. The pungency of bourbon lingering about his warm body was somehow intoxicating as he reached to embrace her. In the near twilight of slumber, his fingertips would touch her so gently, as though she, too, was a delicate instrument to be explored for endless possibilities of sensuous pleasures—from the overture of desire to the finality of the rapturous crescendo each was capable of experiencing.

At the beginning it seemed an imposition to relinquish their day of relaxation, but Sundays soon became another day apart. The customer line at Sally's increased weekly, and there was no going backwards at Pete's—if only for the increased sales of bloody Marys!

Without Sally's presence, Alex was thrust into baking. Even with years of experience, it was difficult to duplicate her mentor's technique. Sally never measured her ingredients precisely, relying instead on how the batter looked and felt. It was similar to reading music compared to playing by ear, and Alex had been trained to read every note.

After studying the recipe cards countless times, she had memorized them in their entirety, even the soiled spots left by Sally's buttered fingers. The initial desserts were acceptable—good enough to sell. But Alex could taste the difference. She had used the same combination of ingredients in the same order, but perhaps the tenseness of her hands or the force of the whisk had betrayed the delicate lusciousness of Sally's originals.

It was a frustration not endured since her omelet crisis in culinary school. She vowed to outsmart those damn stupid eggs —and with practice, she eventually did.

But it was wearing. Alex returned home in the late afternoon, quite ready for a bath and a lounge chair.

Charlie, in contrast, would be on a high. The stimulation of applause, the very atmosphere where chatter met booze, was like ingesting a drug. He was exuberant with conversation about which celebrities came by and all the gala of the day. Alex listened as politely as possible for someone who'd stood on her feet for too many hours.

"You should have been there, honey! The crowd went on shouting for my solos; and when Pete did his 'Royal Garden Blues,' the applause wouldn't stop. As a matter of fact, next week we're adding a vocalist—an old friend of Pete's—a woman named Lovey Williams. She's got quite a reputation around the Quarter."

Alex laughed and couldn't help but quip, "What sort of reputation?"

Charlie laughed with her, but never answered the question.

Before long, subdued Sundays became the focal day of the week. Charlie was relieved to have an excuse to quit the hotel bookings. Those short gigs, trying to be heard over the hustling of a buffet line, were unappreciated and not lucrative.

Instead, he eagerly looked forward to Pete's. Each Saturday he'd run through the repertoire, choosing what he hoped would be crowd favorites. With the addition of a singer, he added songs that included a vocal arrangement, insisting they made the number more interesting. Pete, of course, decided on the program, but Charlie was always ready with suggestions. Alex was pleased for him—and for herself.

She could finally create a soufflé magnifique. Without argument, the voluminous froth would emerge, quite like a golden volcano lingering in the glory of a brief but beautiful sunset, before condensing into its tinfoil container. Sweet to one's taste, everlasting to one's memory, only to have its remains tossed into a nearly receptacle.

With renewed confidence, Alex experimented with new flavors: Kahlúa crème, cherry berries, and even a mint julep that became a favorite with the college crowd.

Yes, Sundays were working out well, but as months passed, the day seemed to stretch into evening. What had begun as Pete's Playtime encroached into nighttime. Alex dawdled at Sally's because she knew Charlie would still be at the club. He'd often—and defiantly—say that the Brunch Bunch (as he jokingly referred to them) wouldn't leave, pleading for just one more, and as long as those bartenders stayed busy, Pete stayed open.

That was the explanation she got as each Sunday expanded. But there was no explaining Charlie's gradual change in mood. He was coming home later and more exhausted each week. Too disinterested to converse, he seemed nearly withdrawn, only wanting something quick to eat before going into their bedroom—alone. Not waiting for Alex to follow, he'd fall into a sleep so deep she listened for his breathing. At first Alex worried that he was ill and, despite strenuous objection, insisted that he get a thorough checkup. When all the tests were complete (including the doctor's advice about a healthier lifestyle—which Charlie ignored), another concern occurred to her: perhaps this sudden fatigue was his way of avoiding conversation. A convenient excuse to explain what was going on.

There was an easy solution to her perplexity. The following week Alex told Sally she wouldn't be available for Sunday duty. But she didn't tell Charlie. She gave him a half-hour lead, then headed for the club, arriving just as he entered the darkened stage. Instead of taking her usual table, Alex sat toward the back, with a clear view of the piano. Pete grabbed the mike, motioning for the boisterous audience to listen to his introduction. In a gravelly voice he boomed his greeting: "Brothers and sisters, welcome to our club today. For your enjoyment we have a special guest artist. A song stylist so scintillating, so captivating, you're gonna love her! In fact, that's her name. New Orleans's favorite: Lovey Williams!"

Thunderous approval roared through the packed-to-capacity room. Charlie had been right: Lovey had quite a reputation. The drummer pounded a throbbing rhythm as a spotlight focused on center stage, worthy of a grand entrance. A woman entered slowly, reveling in each moment's adoration.

Lovey was anything but lovely. She was not young; she was not slim. Quite to the contrary, she was, shall we say, round in all the right places. Her skin was the color of warm honey and despite her years still looked silken to the touch. Under the harsh lighting and concealing makeup, her face reflected years of struggle; of taking what she needed, not to be unkind, but to survive. Her entire essence spoke of a private sadness. Here was a woman who had experienced life from its heights and depths —and sang of it all. When in a sultry tone she longed for her "Lover Man," you knew she'd lived every word of the lyrics. Lovey radiated a beauty unique to herself. She had, indeed, earned her name.

The audience—including Alex—sat mesmerized.

The set concluded with Charlie's signature "Fly Me to the Moon." But instead of his usual solo, Lovey blended in. It was apparent they had merged into one. Their shadings of each note, their subtle nuances evolved into a single instrument as they shared their intimacy with those who watched transfixed.

Even from across the room Alex could read Charlie's expression as Lovey caressed a phrase, knowing her inflection was intended for him. The audience was quiet, respectful. But Alex knew this was not a performance. She felt sick to her stomach and numb. For the past months she'd wanted to believe his alibi about staying late at the club. But she could no longer lie to herself; it was too blatant, too obvious that she had been replaced by someone who sang his language.

What he did and where he went was inconsequential; perhaps it was the hotel across the street, until he was too depleted to be of any good to his songbird.

Alex tried to rise, but her legs wouldn't allow her. They had turned to granite. She tried again, this time pushing against the table's edge for leverage. She was up and free to leave. Joe the bouncer looked at her quizzically as he hailed a taxi. She could only reply that the noise was too much. But even as she reached home, the tumultuous pounding resonated in her head.

Too shaken to do anything else, she sank into a chair and stared at the door, anticipating Charlie's entrance. She didn't have to wait long. Within minutes Charlie burst in, looking as though he'd run all the way. He spoke first.

"Joe told me you were at the club—and you rushed out of there before we were finished. Why didn't you tell me you were coming? Did you come to spy on me? What the hell did you think you'd find?"

Alex sat rigid. She feared any reply would trigger tears and she couldn't allow that to happen. Her silence added to Charlie's anger. "I looked like a fool in front of everyone! I cut out before the encore. Pete and the guys were all asking questions."

"And did Lovey ask you, too? Or did she figure it out all by herself? Surely she's been in this position before!" Alex could finally speak, venom frosting each word.

For a flash Charlie glared at her with an animosity he'd never before revealed. His eyes turned to icicles that thrust through her. A shiver of fear flashed across her shoulders, but Alex remained erect, knowing she could not let down, she could not allow her adversary to win. This time she would respond with control.

"We've both been wrong, Charlie. I should not have come tonight. You should not have given me reason to. Let's go to bed. Nothing can be resolved when we're this tired. Tomorrow we'll be less angry, more reasonable."

Her words were well spoken. They seemed to defuse Charlie's wrath, and he instantly softened, returning to his usual gentle demeanor. Surprisingly, they both slept well. Perhaps it was a welcome escape from reality. But it helped.

Alex called Sally the next morning to say she'd be late, which gave her the opportunity to sit across the table as Charlie had breakfast.

"Listen, baby, I'm sorry I lost my temper last night, but you've got to understand, Lovey and me—we're just friends. There's nothing going on but music."

"Charlie, don't do this to me. I was there, I could feel the connection between the two of you. So please don't deny what we both know."

He flashed Alex an apologetic smile and took a sudden interest in the contents of his coffee cup.

After a good night's rest Alex had resigned herself to the undeniable: Charlie was playing more than the piano.

There was no point in arguing; Alex tried a different approach. "Well, you can't blame me for being a bit jealous, Charlie. I just wanted to see for myself."

"See what, Alex? Tell me, what did you expect to see?" His voice began escalating into the anger of the previous night. Alex quickly backed off.

"Charlie, try to calm down. You and Lovey share a passion in your lives I cannot be part of. I get that."

"But you can be a part, hon. Every time I've wanted you to come with—to be part of what's important to me—you've found some excuse: I'm so tired, Sally needs me, the soufflés need me, everything needs me but Charlie!"

It would have been easier to shout back, louder, more vehemently. But Alex chose instead to confront his allegations with calm.

"I'm sorry, Charlie—for both of us. I came here with all intentions of having a good life with you. I wanted to be your best friend. But I forgot I owed a dignity to myself. Charlie, please understand, I've spent so many years finding out who I am and what I'm worth, I couldn't let that go—even for you. My work at Sally's is just as important to me as your creativity is to you. Please don't malign it or make less of all I'm struggling to be. You constantly need applause. Maybe Lovey can satisfy your insatiable hunger. I tried, I really gave it my best, but it just wasn't enough."

It was over. There were no options. The only problem now was how to conclude graciously for the preservation of Alex's dignity and Charlie's ego.

The next weeks became a game of who could be more courteous. Charlie stayed around, even offering to help with household tasks. Alex canceled out hours at Sally's, preferring to prepare elaborate meals for Charlie's friends. They functioned in an artificial lightness. Often embellished with a pretense of laughter, it was the perfect cover-up of a perfect storm.

When it struck, it did so with intensity. One afternoon, when beams of sunlight floated through the windows illuminating the front rooms of a small yellow house with brightness, Alex told Charlie she was leaving him. Half dressed for his night at Pete's, he stood very still, almost solemn, as he heard the anticipated decision.

"I won't be here when you come back. I'm catching a red-eye home. Back north, where I should be."

Charlie could only nod in agreement. Oddly, as if he hadn't really heard her, he continued to select a tie (her favorite, blue striped) and slip on the shoes near the bed. Alex began to repeat herself, confused by his distraction.

"Charlie, it was wonderful for me, and I loved being in New Orleans with you. But we both know I should leave now so when we think of what we've had together we can smile." Charlie finally stopped dressing and walked slowly toward her, taking her hands in his.

"You know I can't go with you," he said softly. "I've made a life here. But you're different. You belong to the world you understand. We had quite a run, Allie. I remember you telling me you wanted to dance on a silver moon. Well you did, baby. You ran all the way 'round and danced in the glow of those moonbeams."

He studied every detail of her face, knowing he would not see her again. "Now it's time for you to go back to Earth."

Alex felt his kiss, the tenderness of an embrace too sweet to ever be forgotten. She stayed in his arms for a small eternity, then turned and left the room. Minutes later the front door closed behind him, followed by the sound of a car driving away.

Bags packed, Alex called a taxi a half hour too early. She wanted extra time to stop by Pete's Place. Careful to avoid being seen, she waited until Joe was busy checking IDs and then slipped through the door to stand inconspicuously in the shadows. The music blared triumphantly, as if to declare to the world, "Pay attention, this is important." Charlie, seated at his piano, lost to time and place, was completely absorbed in the only love to whom he could be faithful: Music.

It was an indelible picture and Alex breathed it into her very being. It would have to last for the rest of her life. Someone toward the front of the room shouted to Charlie, requesting he play something special. Usually Pete would not allow such a random request, preferring to continue with the set program. But for some reason he agreed, and Charlie began his favorite. Alex glanced at her watch. She had to leave. The meter on the taxi was ticking. A plane was waiting. She captured one final glimpse of Charlie as he played the refrain. Alex whispered softly, "Fly to the moon, dearest Charlie, fly to the moon and play among the stars."

He would not hear her wish him all that he could wish for himself. Though the band played on, her dance was over. Her silver moon had tarnished.

13

A FRESH BEGINNING

The air was crisp and cold—biting at her nostrils. Alex welcomed the chill as an old friend greeting her return home. She turned up the collar on her coat as she approached the taxi. It felt good to recite the condo's address and fumble in her purse for the front-door key. The ride seemed to take too long, especially since the early-morning traffic had not yet begun. Anxious and excited, Alex stared out the window, reacquainting herself with landmarks. Most were there, with the exception of a fast-food place and the frequently displayed "Road work ahead" signs along the way.

Look at me city. I've come back! She thought. But it seemed it had never noticed her absence.

Alex wondered—no, worried—how her home would look, whether the renter had taken care as promised. The young woman had been responsible, paying promptly. Wistfully, Alex thought about those checks. She would miss them. But nothing was going to cloud her homecoming today.

The taxi driver was well rewarded for hauling a multitude of luggage through the lobby, up the elevator, and down the hall. Red-faced, he got only as far as the condo doorway, assuming the lady could drag each piece to the bedroom or empty the contents right there. He didn't care. Alex didn't care either. She had returned, and home had never felt so good! A quick survey reassured her that the rooms had been well kept. There were a few stains on the carpeting, and the soft throw pillows needed to be thrown, but thankfully, everything was just as she'd remembered.

Alex looked at her watch. Too early to call anyone. It had been such a long night of traveling that she hadn't realized the sun was still struggling to make its appearance. Now where was that coffee pot, and was there any coffee to make? After a futile hunt through vacuous cupboards, Alex gave up the search, deciding to take a short nap before rejoining the day.

Throwing a sheet over the mattress cover, she lay down for what was presumed to be a twenty-minute rest. But the emotional impact of the previous night took effect, and it was nearly noon before she awakened. Startled with her new surroundings, she bolted upright, still a bit groggy. Her eyes swept back, then forth across the room as if to confirm her arrival.

The unpacking could wait. The luxury of a shower could not. Oh, how good it felt to immerse herself in a waterfall of warmth, each tiny drop prickling at her skin: *Wake up Alexandra, begin again.*

Clean but hungry, she dressed hurriedly and headed downstairs. As promised, her reliable mechanic had delivered the car he'd been storing during her absence. It had just been washed and stood ready to transport Alex on the day's errands.

The neighborhood had somehow become more attractive, the boulevards wider, the trees majestically raising their branches to become a canopy for all who walked beneath.

Staples acquired, Alex returned to her condo, stocked the barren kitchen with ingredients, and made herself that long-awaited coffee. Delicious. Perhaps not as exotic as a chicory brew (served with powdered-sugar beignets), but the aroma of mocha steaming toward her was quite enough. She grabbed some cheese and a few crackers and opened the small carton of salad from the market. It wasn't as good as the combination she could have made, but it was convenient for now.

There were phone calls to make. David, of course, would be first.

He'd probably be at work, considering the earlier time zone, but Alex didn't care. He wouldn't mind being disturbed by good news. The phone rang only once; apparently David was between meetings.

"Surprise, my darling, it's your mom," was all Alex could utter before he interrupted her with an urgent "Is everything okay?" Alex took a minute to smile as her son spoke his mother's line.

"Yes, David, I'm just fine. I hope I didn't upset you by calling the office, but I wanted you to be the first to know."

"Know what, Mom?" Alex envisioned her son turning pale, so she quickly continued.

"I've come home, dear. Charlie and I ... we split up, and I left him in New Orleans. I've come home." She repeated the words —not so much for David's benefit as to hear them for herself. She liked their sound.

"I'm relieved, Mom. You had a helluva time, and now you're back to the reality that's right for you—where you should be." Not a word was mentioned about Charlie or how he was doing. David was too overjoyed with his mother's decision to care. "Listen, Mom, I've got work to do. Why don't we talk later when I'll have more time?" They said their goodbyes with promises to call soon and sentences ending with love.

Alex had hardly put down the phone when it started to ring. Apparently someone was anxious to reach her.

"Checking on you, baby. You got home alright?" Charlie

sounded concerned. Perhaps it was partly guilt. At any rate, he wanted to know that Alex was safe.

"Yes, Charlie, I'm in the condo, sitting in my favorite chair, sipping coffee."

"I can see it all, Allie. I see you there as if I were with you."

"You'll always be with me, Charlie, you know that." Silence. It was getting too heavy. Charlie needed an escape route, so in character, he quipped, "Great title for a song. I'll have to write it someday." They both laughed and, after a little talk about nothing in particular, found excuses to end the conversation.

Alex put down the phone and sat very still, working to convince herself that she had made the right decision—the only one she could have made to sustain herself.

Within a week the euphoria of being home was replaced by practicality: how to pay the bills. Charlie had been doing so well that he'd insisted on supporting the household, allowing Alex to put most of her income into savings. Looking back, she questioned whether it was generosity or anticipation that this time would come and he could buy himself out of all responsibility. Alex would never know his intent, but she was relieved to stare at a healthy bank statement. Without a job, she'd need that money.

The days became a bittersweet vacillation between missing the free-spirited life in New Orleans and appreciating the steadiness of each repetitive day. She turned on the sound system, loud. Horns and percussion blasted through the quiet with brilliant audacity. The piano had been returned, and the alcove remained vacant. But those melodies had ended, and no recordings could replace the lushness of an artist at play.

Alex began to dream about returning, forgiving Charlie, and trying again. In daylight, though, when she was in full control, she would not allow herself this indulgence ... as much as she longed for his presence and the little yellow house, it was over. Time to move on. Eventually the dreams disappeared from her slumber.

Her days were too full to allow distraction; she needed to find a job. Everything was going out, and not enough was coming in. David tried to calm her with reminders that the annuity was secure and he could add a small check each month.

"I'm starting to do well, Mom. I can skim something off the top until you get situated." Sensing her discomfort, he quickly added, "You'll reimburse me when you can."

"Oh, David, I haven't come to that yet! Thanks for being so thoughtful, but I can't, I won't impose."

He knew he couldn't push harder, but privately he calculated the amount he'd be able to contribute.

Alex procrastinated; it was not a comfortable call. She had left Northridge College abruptly, disappointing Dr. Benneton and the culinary program. Although, he had wished her well with his usual kindness, he had not tried to contact her since. Now she was back, hoping her absence would be overlooked and her employment reinstated. Each day she thought of another excuse to delay, but finally one morning she grabbed her cell and called the familiar number before she could lose courage. A youthful voice answered, "Dr. Benneton's office. May I help you?"

This was not Amelia, but the new assistant was pleasant and agreed to put the call through. Alex swallowed hard. It would be a tough sell, she knew. But oh, how good it was to hear the warm hello of an old friend!

"Alex, my dear, how have you been? Welcome! And how was your time in New Orleans? I've heard splendid news about Charlie and that television series coming out soon. We were sorry to lose him in the music school, but it's not surprising. Someone with his talent tends to move on. So now what can I do for you?"

Alex plunged forward. "Dr. Benneton, I'm home to stay. I've come back from fantasyland and I'm the old Alexandra again and ... I'd like very much to teach culinary classes."

There was an abrupt silence that made Alex more nervous. She gave it her best: "I've learned about other cuisines, Creole and Cajun and —" But she was cut short by the dean's response.

"Alex, you don't have to convince me. I know what an asset you were to the students. I wish I could tell you we have an opening. But your position's been filled by a fine fellow who's doing a good job. The whole department is running well. I'm sorry, I'm so sorry, Alex. I'd be glad to write you a letter of reference. You know I've always admired your ability, and we still boast about Garrett's Garage."

Alex smiled, remembering that sweet summer and the unique restaurant they created. "Well, let's keep in touch, Dr. Benneton. Perhaps lunch sometime."

"I'd like that. You know I'm always here for you. Best of luck, Alex." There was wistfulness in his final words. Alex put down the phone. It had been worth a try, at least. Now what was she supposed to do?

She had made one difficult call, so what did she have to lose making another? She looked at the clock. It was nearing noon Eastern time. She'd take her chances. The phone barely rang before he answered. It must have been in his pocket—or on the seat of the golf cart.

"Well, what a surprise! Alexandra! How the hell have you been? Still in NOLA with the jazz man?" Ted's happy voice boomed through.

"I'm good and I'm home, Ted. It was just a lark. A flight on a gossamer wing, darling."

"You always did have a poetic way, Alex."

They both laughed. "To what do I own this unexpected pleasure?" he asked.

"Well, first of all, Ted, how have you been? What's new?"

"Still on the front nine, honey. My game's not improved, but, get this, I'm a grandfather. My oldest girl, Beth, has a little girl of her own. Her husband manages a hotel in Naples."

"So do you get to see them often?"

"Jean would like to drive over every weekend, but ..."

Alex did not have to inquire about his wife. Apparently she was the same: very much there. After more catching up, Alex got to her concern. "I'm worried, Ted. What can I do to make money?"

"I could tell you it was foolish to give up that position at Northridge—but, of course, you already know that. It was a long shot to go off with that musician character."

Alex so enjoyed hearing the tinge of jealousy in Ted's voice. But it didn't help to resolve her problem.

"Ted, you're the world's smartest entrepreneur. Think of something!"

"Relax, honey. Think of the obvious: apply to a restaurant or start your own catering company."

Alex groaned. "Oh, Ted, I can't risk the capital to start a business, and being a full-time chef is too demanding at my age. I can't stand on a hard kitchen floor for so many hours or lift all those heavy trays. You're remembering the energetic younger woman I once was."

There was the slightest dip in Ted's voice, though he'd never admit to a sigh, as he replied, "And I always will."

Touching as the moment was, they quickly refocused: "I did have one idea that might work: In the New Orleans French Market I helped make fabulous soufflés for a woman named Sally. Tourists just loved them."

"Well what are you waiting for? Write a cookbook, Alex! Include all the cultural flavor of the city, the history of the people's cuisine. Feature Sally's soufflés. Everyone will eat it up. No joke intended."

"Don't tease me, Ted. Do you think it will sell?"

"I'll buy the entire first printing, hon. You've got such expertise, some publisher will grab it."

Alex was chagrined she hadn't thought of a cookbook before; it was such a natural step. With Ted's endorsement, the idea took on a new impetus. Had her earlier years of self-doubt diminished her? She had come too far to allow anything to curtail her now!

"Ted, I knew you'd help me!"

"How many times have I told you, Alexandra? I'm only on the sideline, cheering you on. All this innovation, this creativity, belongs to you. Now run with it, beautiful."

Alex grinned until her face couldn't stretch further. The support was well taken, but his last word was most cherished. To him she remained beautiful.

With obvious spontaneity Ted blurted, "I'm glad you're back, Alex. It bothered the hell out of me that you were living with that piano player. I know we haven't been together for years but I still feel the same ..."

"I know Ted, I've always known."

Silence. The poignancy of silence. Both touched by words that remained unspoken. After a moment, Ted managed to resume his composure and they continued with brief comments and the sincerest intentions to call again soon, Alex and Ted closed with "Goodbye." How often they had said that word without meaning it.

She spent the rest of the day imagining what recipes to include, which pictures to use from her library, and how to draft a letter of consent to Sally. Certainly Alex would develop her own variations, but the basic formula and special techniques belonged to her friend. Alex hoped Sally would allow a photo of herself in her pink-sequined baseball cap, her mouth firmly closed.

It was late when the phone rang, but it was no matter: the

caller was so welcomed.

"David, my love, how nice to hear your voice."

"I should have waited until our usual Sunday, but I've been thinking about you and just wanted to know what's going on."

"Well, I do have news. I've decided to write a cookbook." (Alex could not, of course, disclose that it was Ted's idea.)

"Sounds great, Mom. You've got ten thousand recipes to offer the world!"

Alex chuckled at the thought. "I've even got the title: *The South May Rise Again—Soufflés of New Orleans.*"

The neighbors could have heard David's laughter.

"Clever title, Mom. It's sure to grab attention in a bookstore and online, too."

They continued talking about the new venture, but despite his enthusiasm David's practicality surfaced.

"The book's got to take two years, maybe more, to compile. Remember all the research and development required for your TV show? You spent a zillion hours trying new recipes, perfecting every detail. Where's the money coming from for ingredients? Are you planning on eating wilted soufflés for dinner? Do you know an editor who will work for free? How about pitching it to a publisher? That could take a while."

It was not what his mother wanted to hear. "Oh, David, don't be so discouraging. You just said it was a fine idea."

"I did and it is, Mom. But you have to be realistic. As your self-appointed accountant, I look at the balance sheet. What do you plan to do before this book hits the market? You can't live on invisible royalties."

Alex's soufflé sank. Her voice collapsed as surely as a foamy floss deflates.

"You're right, darling. I was so intrigued I didn't think it through. I still need a job to augment my income; I just don't know what I can do. Who will hire someone my age?"

"Mother, knock it off. You're a valuable resource! You need to figure out specifics. Get some rest. It'll happen."

Alex agreed. Tomorrow was time enough to devise a plan. Tonight she would dream of her son's voice wishing her success.

14

WELL-SEASONED WORDS

The employment agency was across town. It didn't have a street address, only a series of numerals indicating east and west. With the guidance of her GPS (and instructions from the receptionist beforehand), Alex managed to find the office. It was a large, uninteresting room consisting of multiple cubicles containing agents talking incessantly to clients. A young woman approached Alex, extending her arm in greeting. "Hello there, you must be Ms. Silvers. I'm Holly Henderson. Nice to meet you in person. Please follow me."

Before Alex could reply, she was weaving through a maze of modular cubes until Holly stopped, instructed her to sit, and asked how she could be of help. Alex referred to her résumé and began to discuss details, only to be interrupted. It was obvious Holly was on a tight schedule, and the prospect for a commission from placing an older woman was not promising.

"You have extensive experience, Ms. Silvers. Have you considered being a personal chef or managing a retirement-home kitchen? I do have some openings in each."

Alex couldn't see her own expression—but Holly could, and it wasn't good.

"No, I can't be on some family's household staff, and I'm afraid working fifty hours a week at a senior center would be too much for me." Alex attempted to joke, "I'd look too much like a resident."

Holly didn't smile. She probably agreed. She rose from her chair, which gave Alex no other option. Apparently the interview was over.

"Goodbye, Ms. Henderson. Please let me know if anything suitable comes in."

For a flash the two women looked at one another, not just to be polite but to understand where each had come from and, hopefully, where each was headed. Holly was impatient to succeed, and Alex grasped at past achievements to forge a future. Each shared empathy for the other.

Alex couldn't help but feel dejected. That evening she sat with a paper scored in half—one side expenses, the other her income. If she lived frugally, drinking cheaper wine (which is sometimes just as good!) and buying only what she needed (even if it was on sale), she could manage. With that reassurance, she relaxed and called David.

"Mom, don't worry so much. Something will turn up. Meanwhile, you know you can get along. I promise I'll never let you live under a bridge!" From childhood David had known how to cajole her into a better mood. Tonight he had once again done his job well. She slept soundly.

The next day, with a sudden burst of energy, Alex decided to scour the condo as if it were on a house tour. The freshly washed windows accented the luster of polished wood and sparkling crystal lamps. She stood back, admiring the magic of a dust cloth—so lost in thought that her phone rang several times before she realized it. Nearly tripping over the vacuum, she missed the call but got Holly on voicemail.

"Ms. Silvers, give me a call. I might have something for you."

Alex interrupted, "I'm here, Holly. It's me talking!" But Holly had already hung up. After fumbling for the business card tossed somewhere on the dresser, Alex hurriedly pressed "last call" with fingers trembling as she waited for a response.

"Well, hello, Ms. Silvers. Glad to hear from you. I've got a good lead on a job. In fact, I went ahead and set an appointment for you. I hope you can make it."

Alex grabbed a pad from the nightstand and scribbled the necessary information. "I'll be there tomorrow, and thank you. Thanks so much."

At ten o'clock the following day Alexandra Silvers, at her most attractive best, was welcomed into the office of Suzanne Fairfield, publisher of the downtown weekly newspaper. Part business news, part social, it had been in circulation for years and enjoyed a solid reputation. Located in a landmark building on a crowded commercial street, its offices were large to accommodate a staff of editors, reporters, and a sizable art department. Alex was impressed, especially when she was escorted into Ms. Fairfield's private suite.

Unlike Holly, Suzanne was as cosmopolitan as her publication. Tall even without her designer shoes, Suzanne nevertheless retained only the suggestion of the youthful beauty she (and others) had once enjoyed. This attribute had since been upstaged by the elegance accomplished by one who had matured with graciousness. David would have called her a class act. Her manners were equally refined as she greeted her guest.

Alex sat directly across the desk and considered gazing at a panoramic view of towering buildings. It was tempting to look out, but what was being said was too important to be diverted.

"I read your résumé, Ms. Silvers; quite impressive." Suzanne stopped to smile, which reassured an anxious Alexandra. "Tell me about yourself. You've had so many interesting experiences, Ms. Silvers."

"Please call me Alex. Everyone does." New Orleans was an easy conversation. Anecdotes about Sweet Sally's were great icebreakers, and within minutes the two women were talking as warm friends. It was easy to see why Suzanne was successful. Beneath an affable exterior she exuded a strength and astuteness. It was Alex's turn to be impressed. Before long the chatting turned to business.

"We're adding a new feature; I need someone to review restaurants in the area. We're not confined to downtown, even though that's our main circulation. The span would encompass the suburbs as well, and even outlying communities. The column would be featured in our weekend edition each Friday. The salary would be modest until we see reader response, but"—Suzanne laughed—"you'd eat well. Would you be interested, Alex?"

The word yes had never been spoken so quickly. It was agreed. Alex would come in for training the following Monday. Her first critique would run two weeks after. The managing editor would start her off with a list of popular eateries, but after some experience she and staff members would decide on which cuisine to review.

Alex felt competent. She had been eating all her life and, after the experience of composing Charlie's reports for Jake's show, describing food should be easy. She smiled. Her expressions would be "well peppered." Alex did not want to overdo her thank-you, so she extended her hand, smiled broadly, and left Suzanne's office without (hopefully) exposing how much she needed the work.

Her watch showed noon approaching; midmorning on the coast. Probably a busy hour for David. Too bad. She'd call anyway.

"David, I've got great news!"

"Tell me fast, Mom. I have someone in my office."

Quick and concise the words tumbled out, interspersed with something close to a giggle.

Of course David was elated. Alex apologized for interfering. "I had to tell someone—and that someone is you, darling!"

Nice words to end with. David went back to work, and Alexandra stopped by a boutique to buy something new for her first day on the job.

There was another someone to call. It also could come at an awkward time, but Alex was too exuberant to stop. His familiar voice answered in a near whisper. "I'll get back to you," before shutting off. Alex felt embarrassed at her indiscretion. She owed Ted an apology.

Meanwhile, she'd go online to research restaurant reviews. What did the experienced critics say? What was their criteria in granting each star? It made her hungry just to read the commentary and visualize the meal before her. Alex was about to stop and make a sandwich when the phone rang.

"What's new, Alex?" It was Ted in his usual clear voice.

"Oh, I'm sorry to have disturbed you, hon."

"You never disturb me, beautiful. It was just inconvenient. I couldn't talk, but now I can. So, what's going on?"

Alex proudly announced the good news, and Ted was quick to respond. "I want a frequent update on where you've been. I can still remember a few of those restaurants—the ones that have been around forever. Of course, there's a lot of new spots by now. Restaurants are a notorious gamble. So many of them close within a few years that you'll always have new places to review. It's a wonderful job for you, Alex; you worried for nothing. I never would have let you go hungry—now I'm sure you won't."

Ted laughed at his own quip, but Alex continued to ramble

on until it was evident she had said everything twice. At that point, Ted patiently explained he needed to be someplace and closed with heartfelt congratulations and a promise to stay in touch. "If I don't call you, you phone me." The perfect way to leave the door ajar: a commitment without a commitment.

Alex returned to her research, staring at the computer screen, analyzing every critique from competing publications. Some reviewers used a five-star system to rank their opinion. Others simply wrote a reaction to everything from acoustics to the salt on the rim of a margarita glass. Some were kind and forgiving; others could destroy a reputation.

At their first meeting, Alex was not surprised at her new editor's advice: "Put yourself in the customer's chair. What would or wouldn't appeal to them? This is not your personal bias or vendetta. Be honest. Be fair."

A weathered professional, John Kalmer was the ultimate newspaper man. With the sleeves on his striped shirt rolled to the elbows, his tie loosened, and eyebrows furrowed deeply into his forehead, he looked ready to shout, "Hold the presses!" Tough as he appeared, he could be nice when he took a liking to someone. Luckily, he liked Alex, whether he'd been impressed by her extensive background or just wanted to give this older woman a chance to show what she could do.

"Here's your first assignment. Be careful not to disclose your identity. Be an ordinary customer. Take someone with if you like. Fortunately, it's been enough years since your television show that no one should recognize you."

"And I've aged since then."

John actually laughed and replied, "I'm glad you said so and I didn't have to!"

They smiled, knowing they would work together comfortably. John said to call him when needed and wished her good luck.

That was it. Alex was out the door, armed with a healthy appetite and a discerning palate.

Her first venture was a steakhouse in the downtown area. Alex contemplated having dinner alone to get acquainted with the procedure. But, on second thought, it was not the sort of place where a woman would be dining by herself. So she called her longtime friend James Benneton to join her. He was delighted. "Should I pick you up, Alex?"

"No, let's meet there. Remember now, don't give me away!"

"Gracious, no. I'll be the essence of discretion."

Alex was excited. She was about to launch a future career and share it with the best of the past.

When Dean Benneton walked in holding onto a cane for balance, Alex had to look twice. He appeared so much older. The maître d' brought him to the table and, after a warm embrace, the two friends readied themselves for dinner and conversation.

"How good it is to see you, my dear." His face brightened, and his eyes hinted of a little mischief. He had become his younger self once more.

"Order whatever you'd like. Try the appetizers, but save some room for dessert. It's our job, you know!" They explored the menu as if it were a treasure map, careful to be nonchalant when the server approached. They dined for what seemed like hours, Alex occasionally jotting down key impressions to include in her column.

"Oh Alex, it's good to be with you again. You've been missed in the department. All the good you did will never be forgotten. You know, dear friend, I'm retiring after spring semester. It's time. I'm ready to sit around and ..."

"And make pickles!"

Perhaps the timing of the small joke helped divert the mood from becoming too nostalgic. They had shared struggles and triumphs together. Now it was time for gentleness.

"Maybe I'll do that when I return from an extended vacation in England. I've always wanted to visit my ancestral home, even meet some of my long-lost cousins. This will be my chance."

They spoke of their student prodigy, Garrett, who had opened innovative doors in the New York culinary scene. "He's executive chef at some trendy restaurant in Tribeca. How I'd love to review his food! There wouldn't be enough adjectives! We're in touch fairly often. I guess I've become his adoptive mother. It's sweet," Alex exclaimed. Dr. Benneton happily agreed.

With enough wine, the inevitable topic surfaced. Alex went first. "In some way, I'll never forgive myself for going off with Charlie. I'm not a headstrong, impulsive person. I don't know what possessed me. Look what I forfeited; I've had to start over once again. It seems as though I've done that too many times."

Dr. Benneton listened quietly, studying her eyes and the pain they expressed. Finally, when he'd gathered his thoughts, he responded. Instinctively a teacher, he sensed this was not the time for a lengthy lecture.

"You did what made you happy at the time, Alex. Where is it written that you must always be sensible? There's nothing sadder than looking back and saying 'could have, should have.' Do not burden your life with regret, my dear Alexandra, or let anyone—or anything—dilute the harmony you've created. Grasp that sweetness surrounding you, the opportunities, and don't be afraid to begin again. It's exhilarating! Now, let's drink to the future."

Dinner concluded. Alex paid with her credit card and helped the dean to his taxi. Kissing him lightly on the cheek, she tried to express all he had meant to her. But it wasn't necessary. He had always known.

Later that night, alone at her desk, she recalled his wise words. Someday she might need to repeat them to David.

Wrestling with her first review, Alex realized the job was harder than it appeared. At the cost of being negative, she reluctantly described her steak less favorably than expected. Tender, yes, but lacking in special seasoning. The vinaigrette dressing was tart—a welcome contrast to the creamy au gratin potatoes—and a slice of strawberry cheesecake brought a sweet conclusion. The restaurateur should be satisfied, if not elated, with her praise.

John scanned the copy carefully and, with a few revisions, accepted Alex's first review. She was official, empowered with a list of future eateries upon which to descend.

The column was to appear once a week. That meant at least one dinner every four days, allowing time to write the article, get John's approval, and meet the deadline. Between that schedule and finding time (and energy) to work on her soufflé book, Alex had little leisure. She had morphed into a contented (and slightly heavier) workaholic.

One night, as she dozed off before the ten o'clock news, a thirty-second promo surprised her out of foggy slumber. The long-awaited jazz series was about to debut on the public television channel. Alex was deluged with messages from enthusiastic friends who wanted to alert her. All the time and effort Charlie and the team had invested would finally be presented to an appreciative audience. It would be exciting to witness the past come alive and hear his words become drama. The four ninety-minute segments were scheduled on Mondays, in prime time. Initially Alex thought to tape each show for David. But anticipation was so high that the station made the series DVDs available for preorder. Alex would buy two, keeping one for herself.

The first Monday was the most impressive. A surge of emotion consumed Alex when Charles Coleman was listed (in bold type) in the credits. Pride, of course, though tattered by the spotlight of reality. Subsequent weeks got easier as Charlie's

name continued to be highlighted as a key contributor, especially for the fourth segment, the one filmed in Pete's Place.
Alex squinted, searching for familiar corners and marveling at
the garish marquee luring each passerby to enter and enjoy all
that jazz. Pete looked good, and the band behind him did, too.
The lighting director had been lenient on them, softening the
decadence of late nights and too much booze. Alex could
barely recognize Charlie; half hidden behind the keyboard,
head down, he was, as always, immune to distraction. Lost
between melodic chords, intent on playing music that coaxed
the stars out of heaven. She felt relieved. He was there, just
where she'd left him. Content in his exclusivity.

She forced herself to inspect the screen once more. She had
to know. Yes, Lovey Williams was on stage. Alex begrudgingly
admitted the woman was dynamite, dressed in a deep ruby
gown, her décolleté deliberately low. The satiny fabric shim-
mered under the lights; Lovey would not have missed an
opportunity to shine. She didn't need anything but that voice—
raspy with a side of syrup—to hold the customers captive. Even
the camera lens hesitated to move from a woman aching to be
loved.

Alex deliberated about how—and if—she should contact
Charlie. He deserved to be congratulated for all he'd
contributed (even though his "research" was compiled in a
bar!). A call would be polite. There was no use trying to catch
him awake during the day. She'd wait until club hours.

His cell phone rang repeatedly. At last, a recorded voice
announced that the mailbox was full and could not accept any
more messages. Alex hung up, dejected. She'd have to wait and
force herself to try again, the thought of which nagged uncom-
fortably. Maybe she'd send a note addressed to the yellow
house. But what if he'd moved? Before she could lose courage,
Alex grabbed a printed greeting card. How clever. It would be
one-way communication, just a few sentences of well wishes.

She wrote how proud she was of him and the excellent show. There was no mention of the project they shared or the hours she had contribute to make him look good. After rereading the card to assure herself the message was appropriate, she felt a sudden urgency to get it mailed. The note signified a tangible closure: Charlie, done and finished.

Alex headed straight to the post office. After dropping the envelope in the box for the next pickup, she drove away quite satisfied.

In time her reviews got easier. As in most jobs there was a procedure to follow. Doing her best to be discreet, she'd arrive at a restaurant during peak hours to observe both the service and quality of food. After a while, word got around among the chefs. Though the paper deliberately omitted her photo at the top of the column, Alex began to be recognized. John kidded her about wearing a trench coat and slouchy hat—and carrying a briefcase for leftovers. She was pleased to be teased. It was his way of showing approval.

The kitchen cabinet was her secret criteria; it contained a pharmacy of antacids. Every time she was required to use one the restaurant lost a star.

Although she could not select her targets yet, most cuisines were good. On occasion, Alex had to close her eyes and, glass of water in hand, ingest an animal part she had never before encountered. This was true for flavors as well; she experienced combinations and textures from chefs who considered themselves to be culinary Rembrandts. It was all working out fine. For the first time in a long time Alex felt relaxed, slept well, and ate splendidly.

Ted called every now and then, and she called him whenever there was an amusing anecdote to retell. They managed to keep current—he about golf and grandkids, she about sauces and soufflés. His suggestions encouraged Alex to continue the arduous challenge of compiling a book.

"Be certain to include several descriptions of interesting places. Include shots of Sweet Sally's' Give some historical background—the city's so colorful. Put your reader into the scene as though they're right there with you, hon."

Alex listened to Ted's advice, wishing he, too, were right there with her.

15

A SWEET SURPRISE

The pages of her datebook diminished, torn from their spine to be crumpled and tossed away—eliminating the only credible evidence that a day's activity had actually happened. A basket filled with someone's expended life, making way for tomorrow. Each morning Alex awoke, leafed through her Daily, and set out determined to give it her best. Each night she'd retreat into her bed, modestly confident that she had.

Occasionally, when she was overly tired (or dinner had been too spicy), settling down became difficult and she'd distract herself with meandering back to memories of a quaint little house, repainted over the years to resemble sunshine, and the wondrous music that graced it. She questioned just when the laughter had fallen silent and on which day she'd lost her footing on that silver moon. Drifting back into a drowsy reality, Alex admitted there was only one answer: let it go. Life was too good to live backwards.

"Open the door and stand back, Mother!" David's voice came booming through the phone as forcibly as if he'd been in the next room rather than across the country.

"What are you talking about? What do you mean 'stand back'?" Alex asked in such astonishment she needed to grasp the edge of a chair for support. David took a moment to enjoy a secret chuckle, then explained himself. "Mom, I don't know if you have a direct line to the master of all comptrollers, but I got an answer: a position in the accounting department of the home office opened up, and I was first on the list."

"David, darling, are you telling me you're coming back?"

"Yes, Mom, I'm finally coming home."

Alex translated those words to mean she had just won the largest lottery in the history of America. But she could not tell him for the only sound that emerged was the unintelligible, noise one produces when one is laughing and crying at the same time. Finally, after several minutes of this frenzy, she repeated the sentence.

"You're coming home. Oh, David, I've missed you so. I can't believe it."

"Believe it, Mom. I'm finishing up loose ends here and need to stick around to assist the new hire—and then you won't get rid of me."

"It will be a pleasure. The bed in the den is comfortable enough until you find your own place." Another private laugh.

"Well, there's another part of my surprise, Mom. I'm not coming alone. There's two of us."

"Two? Who's two?"

"Her name is Julie Kline. I've been seeing her for quite a while. She's fantastic, and you'll love her—like I do."

"David, you told me that you're either working or going to the library."

"That's right. But I left out the librarian." David couldn't contain his amusement. He behaved like a young boy hiding candy.

"David Silvers, what and who are you talking about?" Alex nearly shouted into the phone.

"Calm down, Mother. Take it easy. When I first got out here and didn't have much money—or know anybody—I'd go over to the library and take out a couple of books. After a while I noticed a cute girl assisting people. She smiled a lot and seemed friendly. I liked that, so I kept making up excuses to get her attention. I never knew I was so interested in marine fishery."

They both stopped to laugh. David continued, "Now Julie admits she noticed me, too, and purposely walked near my table every chance she got. Anyhow, after months of playing under cover—excuse the pun, Mom—I asked her out. Just a coffee, but we got along so well and we talked so long it turned into an all-nighter. It's been that way ever since."

Alex stammered, "Why haven't you told me before? What's so secretive?"

"Well, Mom, I just wasn't ready. I wanted to make sure this relationship was real, that we could last together. I watched you and Dad and ..."

"I know, David. And you don't want to repeat our mistake. But no one has insurance for twenty years down the road. If it feels good to you now, just go for it. Enjoy."

"Thanks, Mom. Julie's excited to meet you. She doesn't have much family—only her dad and sister upstate—so she'll love having you."

"I'll do my best, darling. But I've never had to share you before."

"You're not sharing me, Mom. There's enough to go around. I seem to have packed on a few. Julie likes to cook, too." Thinking fast, David added, "But she's not as good as you!"

With that, the conversation came to a natural conclusion. What more was there to say except "See you soon"?

The next weeks were filled with anticipation. Alex contacted her former realtor and requested potential rental properties. David required a range of options. Controlling her opinion was hard, but Alex realized she didn't have a vote. The eventual winner was a loft in the old warehouse district. Renovated from a former garment factory, its walls were weathered bricks with open pipes along the high ceiling. One end of the expansive room had been renovated into a sleek, stainless-steel kitchen. An area rug covered the concrete floor to define the bedroom corner. It wasn't to Alex's traditional taste, but it didn't matter; she welcomed returning to the formality of her own home.

The doorbell was jarring. It was past midnight when two very tired travelers appeared in Alex's doorway.

"What are you doing here? I didn't expect you until tomorrow!" Alex blurted out, fumbling with the sash on her robe.

"Sorry to surprise you, Mom, but we got a chance to go standby so we grabbed it—and here we are!"

They trudged in, dragging enough suitcases that the hallway soon resembled a hotel lobby.

Alex immediately asked if they were hungry. David, anticipating such a question, replied, "Starved." But before she agreed, arms were extended and mother and son embraced in an exuberant welcoming hug. Suddenly they both remembered Julie, who stood observing the other woman in her partner's life. Not waiting for an introduction, the two women clasped hands, both exclaiming simultaneously how happy they were to finally meet. It was a bit over the top, each trying hard to make a good first impression. Fortunately, David broke into their gushing.

"I'll show Julie around, Mom. We'll make up the den and crash here for the night. Tomorrow we'll check out our new pad." Alex was relieved to exit into the kitchen, leaving her unexpected houseguests to settle in. Tomorrow would be time enough to get acquainted. This night (or what was left of it) was meant for sandwiches and sleep.

Conveniently, Alex had a table reserved at a newly opened French bistro for that Saturday night and her dining allowance entitled her to bring guests. It would be perfect for conversing between l'oignon gratinée and crepes au Grand Marnier. David ate while the two women got to know each other. Julie spoke of her family and how she'd worked her way through school to earn a master's degree in library science. Every so often David interrupted to add some academic title she'd won. Julie would then fumble with the napkin on her lap, embarrassed, but pleased as well. It was obvious they were proud of each other.

Although Julie didn't look the part—David had always been attracted to the blonde du jour—Julie's presence radiated a kindness all her own. By Hollywood standards, she was merely a sweet somebody immersed in the crowd, not stunning enough to turn heads. But here was a young woman of quality whom David could trust with his future. Skeptical at first, Alex sat back, reassured. Julie Kline was worthy of her son. An honor well earned—and thoughtfully bestowed.

The following days were a scramble of activity. Mother again helped son to shop, only instead of school supplies they purchased shower curtains and wastebaskets. Equipping the new apartment was time consuming, but Julie had a requirement that took precedence over lampshades. Applying to libraries around the city, she'd often have two interviews in a day, then wait anxiously for a call back. During this tense time she pulled into her private cocoon for comfort. After what seemed like an eternity (but was actually only weeks), the right position in the area of choice was offered, and she accepted.

David, already familiar with procedures from the West Coast office, adjusted well to his new position.

Alex continued her column, sometimes even extracting a comment edging on a compliment from stoic John. This approval entitled her to a substantial year-end bonus. The honeymoon period was appreciated, but Alex knew it was only a fleeting camouflage for the fireworks that would inevitably ignite. Life does not stay on vacation.

16

RIGHTING THE WRITING

One New Year's Eve merged into another. Flutes of champagne were barely emptied before being filled again to toast yet another year. David and Julie were happy, so Alex was happy and productive. It was a time when she relaxed in a capsule of complacency. Life as she knew it was behaving.

The soufflé book had swelled to voluminous pages. It was taking far longer than planned to complete, for each recipe or vignette encouraged another. Alex joked that it was her "self-rising flour."

Inexperienced in creative writing and unsure about where to put a semicolon, Alex desperately needed an editor, so she made an appointment with Suzanne Fairfield.

"Come in, sit over here, Alexandra. What's on your mind?"

Since their first meeting long before, the woman had not aged half a minute. She was sleek and trim and flawless as ever, and Alex consoled herself that a master surgeon must have sculpted her image. But it was hard to resent such a nice person. At home in a bathrobe, she undoubtedly looked like everyone else.

"I've written a book, Suzanne, and it needs careful editing. I can't submit it to a publisher the way it is now. Do you know of anyone to help me?"

Suzanne smiled, relieved. "I thought you were going to resign on me. I'm glad this is what you wanted. I absolutely agree a good editor is vital. People don't realize how they influence the finished copy. I've done some writing myself, so I know firsthand. Let me read the manuscript so that I can find the right person for you."

"I'm embarrassed to have you see all my mistakes," Alex joked. "Remember, I'm a chef, not an author."

Suzanne continued unaware, absorbed in thought. "When I was earning my master's degree I edited PhD theses to pay tuition. It was my first venture into the literary world. I'll look forward to reading your work, Alexandra. It's an achievement to even get this far."

It was the encouragement Alex needed. Leaving Suzanne's office that day, her mood was as high as her pistachio soufflé. But as days passed into weeks, Suzanne did not call. Alex became increasingly anxious and considered phoning her with some flimsy excuse to start the conversation. She controlled the temptation, but as time elapsed that serpent of insecurity coiled into thought. *She probably dislikes the book, but is too polite to tell me. I shouldn't have imposed on her. It wasn't ready for reviewing.* Doubt plagued her, though her better sense told her to quit the dramatics.

Finally, judgment came. "Alexandra! Suzanne. How are you doing? I read your last review about eating goat fricassee at Café Bombay."

Alex wanted to reply, "My heart is about to leave my body. Please get to the point."

"Sorry it's taken me so long to study your manuscript, but I wanted to be careful in my decisions. Congratulations, you have the potential for a very good book. Your background material is believable, and, although I don't cook, the recipes sound delicious. That being said, it needs work—tightening. I asked a few colleagues whom they'd suggest, and I've got a name for you. Hope you don't mind, but I made an initial call so that you could get a referral discount. Here's the info."

Alex fumbled in a kitchen drawer for a pen, fearing she might have to scribble on the back of a grocery receipt. Luckily, Suzanne offered to send an email instead. Alex blurted out, "That would be just fine—and thank you, I can't thank you enough!"

Suzanne, gracious a usual, only murmured, "Much luck on the project" before saying goodbye.

The message that followed contained all Alex needed to proceed. The editor's name was Liz Sherman, on staff at the Lilith Publishing Company, located near the river, not far from Northridge College. She wasted no time in calling for an appointment. The following Wednesday, Alex arrived with a carton of papers at Liz's office. The preliminary meeting was pleasant, to the point, and productive—quite like the editor herself. In her early fifties, Liz had been with the company since its inception fifteen years earlier. Comprised mostly of women (the lone exception being one man in the marketing department), Lilith was a book packager that prepared books for prominent New York publishers. Liz and her assistant dealt with authors preparing their work to sell.

"Ms. Fairfield spoke highly of you, and I've often read your restaurant reviews," Liz said. She had a quick laugh. "But you must remember that describing a meal is not the same as composing an entire book." She patted the manuscript before her. "You can take all this back with you. We'll be working on the computer. Paper copy is obsolete now."

The two women—novice and pro—smiled, sensing their collaboration would go well. "Give me some time, Alex. I'll get back to you with suggestions. Meanwhile, go critique a chicken." Alex had to laugh, relieved that Liz showed a sense of fun.

Later that night, Alex dialed David to relay a detailed account of the meeting. Unfortunately, he'd just come in, hadn't eaten, and was not in the mood to listen. "Sorry, Mom, it's the month ending. I'll call you this weekend."

Balloon punctured, Alex put down the phone, turned on the cooking channel, polished off a bag of cashews, and consoled herself that tomorrow she'd call Ted.

As always, he made time to listen.

"Sounds great, Alex. Your editor can help polish the book. She'll see it more objectively. You're so involved, it's almost become a child to nurture." Ted sounded confident that Alex was making a smart choice.

"I can't wait to send you the finished manuscript. I'm anxious to get your reaction."

"Listen, hon, I'll be glad to read it—and offer my literary expertise." They paused to laugh. "But remember to mail it to my attorney's office. Mac will let me know when it arrives, and I can keep it in my locker at the club."

"Of course, Ted. What would I ever do without you?"

Before he felt pressured to reply, before she could get more sentimental, Alex curtailed the conversation with a safe "Goodbye."

Liz had more than a sense of humor; she contributed keen insight plus a fresh prospective. Many paragraphs had notations. Alex contemplated the suggestions, adopting some new ideas but clinging to her original descriptions by repeating to herself that it was, after all, her book, her baby. But Liz was persistent: "Go deeper, Alex. Pull your reader into the scene like an artist awakening your awareness. We're there, in a brick-walled courtyard, surrounded by sprawling greenery and magnolia blossoms, dining at a white wrought-iron table. A gooey spoonful of warm soufflé teases us to indulge in just one more bite. See what I'm getting at?"

Alex began to doubt she'd live long enough to see the elusive words *The End* appear. But one day, hallelujah, Liz was satisfied. The innocuous stack of papers had developed into a possible book. Alex was jubilant, Liz restrained. "Well, we've got a product. We've made your work smoother, more professional, ready to submit. But as good as we think it might be, a publisher is going to have their own opinion—and editor. Steel yourself: you will probably have to go through this process again if and when it gets published."

Alex sat back, somewhat surprised, but more disappointed. Those two letters *IF* had never entered her mind. In her daydreams, the manuscript would be welcomed unequivocally.

"Oh, Liz, I never realized putting a book together was so complicated. You've done such a good job and ..." Her voice trailed off as Liz studied her tense expression.

"I'm turning this over to one of our best literary agents," Liz said. "She'll know which publishing house to begin with. We'll start with the ones that specialize in cookbooks, or at least have a subsidiary that do, where we'll have our best chance. Listen, Alex, you can't be discouraged by rejection. It usually happens, unless you're a celebrity." She paused for a second before adding, "If only you were a movie star!" The two women, friends that they'd become, couldn't resist a laugh. After months of tedium it felt good. So it was done—for now—and Alex returned, without distraction, to judging lamb chops with mint sauce.

As Liz had warned, the rejections arrived, first from the big, familiar names in publishing. Choices were dwindling. The comments ranged from a polite "It doesn't fit our genre" to "Our agenda is established for this fiscal year." They all wished Alex the best of luck and thanked her for submitting. It was painful. Alex complained to David she'd soon have enough rejection letters to paper a wall. But her son, the indomitable fan, retorted, "Someday Julie will feature it in the library. She'll prop it on an easel right in front, and there'll be a waiting list to borrow it!"

Ted took a different approach. His years in business had toughened him to expect setbacks. Though he had thought the manuscript was interesting, his inability to fry an egg reduced his judgment to total bias.

Months passed, and Alex had a difficult time staying optimistic. Liz offered an alternative to self-publish. But Alex was reluctant to deplete her savings and struggle with the necessary marketing. David offered to help, but he and Julie had just bought a house and Alex couldn't accept their generosity. It was a waiting game with no guarantee of a prize at the end.

"Stop feeling sorry for yourself, Alex. You've put yourself out there before, and look at all the jobs you've done successfully." Ted was emphatic.

Alex rebelled. "But somehow it always worked out."

"You didn't know that at the start, Alex. I've never known you to be so discouraged. Where's that old audacity?"

"Oh, Ted, I've gone through so much!"

"You've gone through so much to be the person you are."

Nothing more needed to be said.

What happened next was pure kismet, or just plain luck: the phone call that changed everything.

"Ms. S., is this you? It's me, Garrett. We haven't talked since too long. I think of you a lot and wanted to know how you've been."

Garrett's voice resonated with confidence, giving him a depth of authority light years past the timid fledging whom Alex had taken under her wing.

"How wonderful to hear from you, dear! You sound happy and I know you've been busy. So many great comments have been printed about your restaurant; it's got quite a reputation. I'm still reviewing, so I'm up on all the latest news."

Garrett's grin could be felt through the phone. "Now tell me what's going on, Ms. S. Have you finally finished that book? If it's ready, I'd love to read it."

"Oh, Garrett, you can't imagine what's happened. My literary agent has been submitting it to publishers, and nobody wants it. I'm crushed!" There was a pause. "Garrett, are you still there?" Alex waited, hearing only an inaudible sound on the line.

"Yes, I'm here. Listen, send me the manuscript. I want to see it. Maybe I can give you some suggestions—find a way to make it more saleable. I've had some luck with a couple of cookbooks, you know."

"Of course, I've got both editions you've sent me. I'm so proud of you."

"So let me take a look and I'll get back to you, my friend."

They moved on to chatting about people and places they'd shared. Sweet times, fond memories. Alex put down the phone feeling renewed. She couldn't wait to tell Liz, but was surprised at her cautious response.

"Alex, I'm delighted to hear about Garrett. I feel I know him from all your stories—such a nice fellow. But don't get ahead of yourself. He can't guarantee a sale."

"I know that, Liz, but I'm flattered he's interested. It can only help to send him a copy."

That was it. Alex tried to let go of all fantasies and concentrate on the weekly business of yet another eatery. Swallowing an overly sticky bun (that adhered to her teeth) and dealing with a whole poached fish (with its eye staring up at her) was, indeed, a strange way to make a living.

17

THE SOUFFLÉ ERUPTS

One morning, too early for the world to know she'd awakened, the phone rang. Alex raced to answer, still half asleep but fearful it was David, lying in a hospital. Of course it was nothing of the sort.

Garrett's voice thundered, "Ms. S., hope I didn't wake you. It's later here. I'm already preparing lunch, and –"

Alex interrupted "For heaven's sakes, Garrett, what is it?"

"We've—you've—got a publisher! The company I do business with. You've heard of them—they're one of the best. I gave it to one of the executives I know. He just got back to me. They liked it and are willing to take a chance on it even though you don't have a national reputation. I'm not yet sure about an advanced royalty but ..."

Alex heard no more because of the choir of angels singing inside her head. All she could say was "I can't believe it" until Garrett gently suggested she take a deep breath. Then he assured her that someone would be in contact soon, There were many details to cover and, best of all, a contract to sign.

David and Julie wanted to share a celebratory dinner, but Alex declined; having tasted every item on every menu in the city (and surrounding areas), she preferred a serene evening at home munching carbohydrates of choice.

The next day Alex called Ted with the triumphant news. He was not that surprised. He had felt all along it was only a test of patience before success arrived. Liz, however, had a different, more restrained reaction. She thought it had all happened too quickly, too slickly. Alex attributed this to professional competition. Lilith Agency, after all, had not made the sale.

Within the week Alex was bombarded with paperwork enough to require consultation with an attorney in David's office. The contract was signed by both parties, and work was scheduled to begin on a second edit provided by the publisher —standard procedure for every investment they made. A woman named Kay Sloane was assigned. Though she lived half a country away, Alex found it easy to communicate with her. Alex surmised from her voice that she was young, but as soon as David helped her Skype, she realized Kay was younger than her son.

"Well, she must be extremely bright to be on staff. Apparently she knows what she's doing," Alex said to herself afterward. It sounded more convincing that way. From day one they were water and oil. Unlike Liz, Kay didn't make small talk. Idle chatter took time away from their work. So Alex refrained from even asking how she was or wishing her a pleasant weekend.

The first time was the worst time as Alex read Kay's negative notes scribbled alongside most paragraphs. *Rewrite this, delete that.* Alex had steeled herself for criticism, but these comments were exceptionally harsh. Garrett kept reassuring her it was customary, but Alex only half believed him. It appeared Kay objected to the very substance of the book. The two women were artistically opposite.

Kay was demanding. "Come on, Alex, this manuscript needs more glitz. It's got to be contemporary to sell; you can't dwell on past history. Talk about now: what's happening on the scene. You need to appeal to a younger demographic—the ones spending the money. They're not serving soufflés in assisted-living centers! Make those recipes current—more veggies, less fat."

As Kay continued her tirade about content, Alex felt she was losing creative control; this was not the book she had conceptualized. Much as she tried to defend her preferences, Kay countered her with objections. It was an explosion waiting to happen.

"Look Alex, I've got a job here. I know what I'm doing, so listen to me—I'm trying to help you!"

Until then Alex had managed to restrain her temper, but one key statement opened a floodgate. All her frustration burst out in a torrent of anger with an undercurrent of animosity. "You've criticized me from the beginning. Everything I've written, every recipe isn't good enough. What the hell is your problem?"

The single shot started a war. Alex had pushed Kay too far. "Listen, I only agreed to edit this because orders came from the top. Believe me, I didn't want to, but I need to keep my job. Are you so naïve as to think they really wanted you—someone nobody's ever heard of? Don't be a fool. Your friend Garrett arranged the whole deal. He had to promise the publisher exclusivity on his next cookbook—the best seller. That's the only reason you're here, lady! I know you won't believe me, but I am trying to whip this book into shape. So let me do my job and get done with it!"

Fortunately, Alex was sitting down as Kay's arrows pierced. It would have been a painful descent to the tile floor. She froze, trying to recall each sentence, not fully cognizant of what she'd just heard. Kay's fury explained her attitude; she had been forced to take on a project she resented. The book was merely a throwaway to get the blockbuster they wanted. In an ironic way, Kay was being used just as she was. A mandatory order from the boss upstairs. Almost humorous, but nobody was laughing.

Strangely enough, their collision was helpful. They each took a deep breath, paused to regain their composure, and went back to work, earnestly trying to grasp the other's point of view. Kay even came close to apologizing. Perhaps it was motivated only by the concern that Alex would go crying to the editor-in-chief. Alex hoped it came from a kinder place.

"I shouldn't have blurted out about that Garrett business, but everyone on staff knows. It's never been a secret, so I assumed you knew, too. Anyhow, thanks for not complaining."

Month after month, Alex revised what she'd written and worked with fresh ingredients into combinations she'd never created before. When she felt like throwing the entire manuscript into a trash can, when she couldn't bear to look at another page without the urge to scream, Kay informed her the book-to-be was ready for the proofreader. Which meant the long-awaited printer would soon follow!

The release date was set for early autumn—prime time for the season's entertaining and holiday gifts. Alex and everyone who cared about her were jubilant, and relieved that the lengthy, laborious project was approaching an end. David, with his numerical mind, calculated that a newborn baby would have entered school in the equivalent time it took to birth this book.

Suzanne Fairfield offered to give a launch reception in the newspaper's dining room. She said she'd keep it simple, but Alex knew it would be a splendid party with hors d'oeuvres and plenty of bubbly. The books would be on display to facilitate purchases and Alex would conveniently be available for a personal signing. How exciting for a new author to have a first book debut! Those thrilling hours would come only once.

Alex enjoyed lingering at the event, but no momentary pleasure would obliterate a decision that could not be avoided.

She had been reticent about speaking to Garrett about his agreement with the publisher. During their next call she alluded to the subject carefully and listened for his response. His discomfort was immediately apparent. Knowing Garrett so well, it was obvious to her why he'd been so generous. To his thinking it was payback for her help those years long ago, when she brought hope to his desolation and recognized potential before he knew he had it. Until now he'd had no opportunity to show his gratitude.

Alex decided some things are better left unsaid. This was one of them.

Liz was a different audience. When Alex told her about the publisher's arrangement, she reenacted Kay's outburst verbatim. Liz sat stone-faced, not at all surprised or dismayed, taking it all in as though she'd heard it before. Apparently she had. When Alex finally concluded her dramatic dialogue, Liz shook her head as if to dismiss the rant.

"Welcome to reality, Ms. Silvers. It's the old 'grab what you can and don't look back.' Run like lightning with it, Alex! Hey, everyone got what they wanted. The publisher's going to make a lot of money with Garrett; he feels good about helping an old friend; and you, my dear author, have a contract an unknown writer would give anything for." Liz paused to smile. "Well, maybe not anything, but you get the idea!" They both had to laugh before switching the subject to the weather.

That left David, who naturally thought his mother could walk on the very water others used for soup. How, Alex pondered, could she break the news of the deal? After much deliberation, Alex waited for a moment of distraction. Just when he was concentrating on driving in traffic, she noted, "By the way, my publisher is Garrett's, too. He helped me secure a contract." Enough said.

David responded. "Good. That's how business works, Mom.

Do I take a left at the next stoplight?" Done. It was off her conscience and out of mind.

Now Alex could concentrate on promoting sales as dictated in the newly esteemed contract. Jason, the lone (and perhaps lonely) male in Lilith's marketing department, called to set an appointment. They needed a strategic plan. With Suzanne's input, the Around the Town columnist would include a paragraph about the book's release, followed by a glowing review from the food editor including the recipe for cranberry soufflé —a light alternative to Thanksgiving's pecan pie. After that, the paper's literary editor would list the book in her "Hot Reads for Cool Weather" article.

Jason arranged for signing engagements at various bookstores and appearances at women's organizations at which Alex would socialize before giving a short review. Déjà vu: she drifted back to fond memories of *Alexandra the Grate* and the many personal engagements a television show required. Perhaps, if there were any personal contacts left at the station, Jason could arrange an interview. She must remember to mention that next time they meet. Enthusiasm bred interest, and, with the skill of a good marketer—and a little help from her friends—it would also breed financial success. Her publisher was pleasantly surprised it had such strong local sales, having taken a wait-and-see attitude before booking Alex into more lucrative markets. Month after month, sales increased as word spread that it was delightful. Alex, half begrudgingly, admitted that Kay had known what she was doing. She declined, however, to send her a thank-you note.

18

A BITE OF THE BIG APPLE

Jason kept in close touch, continually sending complimentary copies to the media. Alex joked that for the first time she was able to buy holiday gifts without imploding her credit card. The royalties were her personal Santa.

The new year came, and as the winter lull approached, sales chilled like the weather. It was to be expected; people were spending their money on health-club memberships. So when Jason called on a snow-swept afternoon, his voice brightened the day.

"Alexandra, I can't work with you any longer." The words were blunt, but his voice held an impish inflection.

"But why, Jason? You've done such an excellent job."

"That I have. I've exceeded myself out of a job. It's time to relinquish your book to the publicist at your publishers. Alex, they're so impressed with what we've accomplished locally that they want to arrange an important signing for you in New York. Congrats, Ms. Silvers, your little soufflé has turned into the Big Apple!"

"Jason, you must be kidding! They didn't want to bother

with me when they thought I was just Garrett's tagalong. What do they want with me in New York?"

"As I've said, their publicist, someone named Brent Fogelson—oh, it doesn't matter—notified me you're to be there in a few weeks for not only a book signing but—and get this—a pre-event with food editors. You'll be interviewed by and hopefully reviewed in various publications. Sounds like a good deal to me, Alex, and in my opinion, you've earned it!"

Jason stopped to breathe. Alex was stunned, capable only of uttering three thank-yous and a request for details. Regaining his composure, Jason offered to help with arrangements as soon as the bookstore's location was known.

For the next hour the phone never left Alex's hand: first a call to David, next to Suzanne, and finally to a number long memorized.

"Hi, Ted. Do you have time? I've got news." He sounded involved—perhaps in a meeting. It was midday in Boca.

"Just a minute. What is it, Alex?" She inhaled deeply and then, without stopping to breathe again, delivered the glorious announcement. Ted listened without comment. When he did speak, it was an unexpected response.

"I can't talk now. But give me the specifics—date and place. I've got some business transactions in the city. I'll try to meet you there. Have to go, Alex. Proud of you, Beautiful."

That was all there was, but Alex had to sink into a chair afterward. On an ordinary day, in the midst of a dreary northern frost, the sky had somehow opened and rays of sunlight shone through. Possibly, with the exception of David's birth, this had become her best day ever on Earth. It wasn't yet five o'clock, but who cared. Bar open!

Jason was quick to communicate the schedule so they could make reservations. Garrett offered to cater refreshments for the interview party. With important food writers attending, it would be good exposure for his restaurant as well as for Alex.

He also suggested a charming hotel near the bookstore—
Chateau Madeleine—that Alex would surely enjoy. Arrangements fell into place, and Ted confirmed the dates were clear
for him. Jean would be in Naples.

"It's been so long since we've been with each other. I hope
you'll recognize me," Alex spoke almost teasingly.

She could hear Ted's amusement as he assured her there
wouldn't be a problem. He would fly in that morning, register
at a midtown hotel, and meet with his business associates until
late afternoon. Alex regretted that he'd miss the book event, but
they agreed it was better he wasn't there. Even in a large
metropolis, someone they both knew could see them together.
They would meet at her hotel by six.

Frequent messages from New York were sent to Jason who,
in turn, relayed the information to Alex. Major newspapers
would place advance advertisements, including a photo and
bio of Alex, and bookstores would prominently display large
signs. Local radio stations were would run spot announcements. Reservations for the party beforehand were encouraging. All Alex had to do was show up and be affable. It seemed
like a dream sequence she was waltzing through: all this, and
Ted, too!

As Alex headed east, an unyielding climate seemed to
follow. There were ominous predictions of storms heading
toward the city within thirty-six hours. Alex's plane landed on
schedule, and she arrived at Chateau Madeleine, an elite
boutique hotel, in the early evening. Garrett had already left a
message about bringing over dinner, allowing enough time for
Alex to freshen up. After checking in, she was escorted to the
corner of floor three. Stepping into the room was passage to a
land of make-believe reminiscent of Versailles fitted with
modern-day conveniences. Walls appliquéd in a palette of ivory
felt silken to the touch. Tiny imprinted butterflies flew freely
along the border. The king-size bed lay luxuriously beneath a

pleated canopy headboard. Draperies, drawn back with braided ropes, guarded the floor-to-ceiling windows. It was a kind of elegance recaptured from another era in time, one long forgotten amid today's sleek technology.

Alex could only imagine how Ted's eyes would encompass such romanticism. But before she could give that much thought, Garrett called to say he was on his way. As excited as she was to see him and hear about the past year, the restaurant reviewer inside her was eager to taste that fabulous food.

The knock on the door nearly knocked her over. There stood the adult version of the boy she'd left behind, full-figured (from being his own gourmet) and showing a hint of gray at a thinning hairline. How could this be her young Garrett? They took a minute to just stare at each other: Garrett the Grown-Up, Alex the Proud Mentor.

"Well, don't just stand there in the doorway! Come in, set the food over on the table."

Garrett put down the insulated box, turned, and nearly smothered her in a hug he only reluctantly released. They both started talking at the same time, not waiting for answers before demanding, "Tell me about yourself." Finally, Garrett suggested they eat dinner. "I brought the house specialty: chicken stuffed with homemade corned beef and provolone cheese, served with a Dijon wine sauce."

One bite convinced Alex why he'd earned coveted awards and his restaurant was booked weeks ahead. Garrett spoke of his triumphs and, yes, his struggles. Millie Mae had OD'd not long after he'd come east, and with few relatives left, he'd been on his own. Putting his career first—and nearly living in commercial kitchens—he'd never made a priority of having a family. But he didn't mention loneliness or regret; this was the life he wanted.

The conversation then turned to Alex. She touched briefly on New Orleans and Charlie, leaving out details. But Garrett, as perceptive as an artist is, heard all the undertones she didn't express: the anger at herself for leaving Northridge, the uphill climb of starting over again. He listened intently, allowing her to unwrap emotions without fear of judgment, and when she was through, when she had emptied herself, he gently wiped away the sadness with kindness.

"You did what you thought was best at the time. That's all any of us can do, Ms. S. You win some, you lose some. Trust me, I know. But you can't live with regret; you just go on."

It was a lovely way to spend the evening. Garrett left soon after, allowing Alex to get a full night's sleep before her triumphant tomorrow.

The sky was foreboding, forecasting an impending storm, but to Alex the day felt sunny with soft undertones of warmth. Perfect timing: stepping fresh from the shower and pulling the complimentary robe around her, Alex dashed for her phone to hear Ted's "Morning, beautiful. Got in town late last night. I'm at the Star Sapphire Hotel, with a full day of meetings ahead."

"Oh Ted, I can't wait to see you! What time, darling?"

Ted hesitated for a moment before declaring that six o'clock sounded about right. He then wished her a successful event and, as always, said he had to be somewhere to meet someone soon.

Alex couldn't decide whether to be more elated about the book signing or being with the man she'd never forgotten. Meanwhile, she was hungry. Garret's luscious dinner was now a memory. As she called room service, she wondered when—and if—she'd have time in the day to eat again. The eggs had barely been tasted when the phone rang for the second time. It was Brent, the publicist, reminding her to be on time and asking if she wanted to be picked up even though the bookstore was only a block away. After listening politely Alex said yes, she'd be prompt, and no, she'd manage to find the place alone. Seemingly satisfied, he wished her well and hung up, leaving Alex to finish her now-cold omelet.

As promised, Alex appeared in the doorway of Booksellers, Inc., six minutes before the requested hour. The staff had everything set: a long table stacked with books and, on each end, a glossy sixteen-by-twenty-inch poster of Alex beaming as she held a copy for all to acknowledge. (Fortunately the photographer from Lilith had been generous with an airbrush!) Recognizing her from the picture, a woman with a chain of jingling beads attached to her glasses approached her. Bustling up, she said authoritatively, "You must be our author, Alexandra. Welcome." Not waiting for a confirmation—or any reply—the manager (as she turned out to be) recited the afternoon's procedure. Initially Alex was to be seated in their Cozy Reader's Nook, available for interviews by interested columnists. Then, at the designated hour, she would move to the long table and, using the set of available pens, write each customer's name and her own signature on the front page of every copy sold. Garrett's buffet table looked wonderful from a distance, but Alex could only wave at it. The store became increasingly busy as announcements were made over the loudspeaker.

Alex sat dutifully, hands folded in her lap, as inquisitive food writers approached her in the Nook. "What else have you done? Did you always love to cook?"

At first she attempted to give details, beginning with her prestigious education at London's Ecole de Cuisine. But soon there was too much to explain, making it easier to recite a four-minute speech of who she was and how she got there. Everyone was pleasant. The entire store was pleasant. But after more than an hour, Alex felt she was descending into Dancing Bear Syndrome: performing for the interviews with witticisms and amusing anecdotes to give the group snappy quotes for their columns. It was a welcome relief when the manager came to escort her to the book table, where a line of women waited to meet and greet.

Other than the fear she'd misspell someone's name, Alex was delighted to chat with would-be chefs. The hours disappeared, and so did the customers. Both the queue and the stack of books dwindled. The Big Event was reduced to memory, to be retold (with added flourishes) in the future.

Alex took a deep breath, knowing the day that seemed over had yet to begin. It was past four o'clock, time enough to revitalize for an evening she'd thought would never happen. After thanking everyone, including the manager (whose glasses now bounced on her adequate bosom, the two strands of beads dangling whimsically as she moved), Alex hurried back to the hotel. She needed to put a cool compress on her eyes and escape to a mellow place. Ted could not see her fatigued.

19

THE ROOM ON FLOOR THREE

J ust after six o'clock, the phone rang. For a split second Alex feared he'd called to cancel.

"Honey, what's your room number? My cab's just pulling up."

Luckily it was the memorable 330, for her mind went blank. "See you" and click. A wave of panic engulfed her.

Before she could run into the hall and hide in the supply closet, or perhaps climb out onto the fire escape, there was a knock on the door. This was it.

Alex looked up and thanked whatever force was in charge of opening the heavens. Then, with a firm grasp, she pulled back the last barrier between her and the man she'd never stopped loving.

Neither moved. They stood silent, smiling, staring in near disbelief that after decades apart, they were finally together.

"Can I come in?"

Alex laughed and stepped aside, and, as the door of room 330 closed out the world, they embraced as if they would never let go.

"You look wonderful, Alex. Not a day older."

"Ted, it's been nearly twenty years!"

"Has it been that long? It's gone so quickly."

Each fibbing a bit to soothe the other's vanity, they accentuated all the good, avoiding the obvious character lines. Sentences began, then halted abruptly to start again, both listening but not really paying attention, seeing but not focusing, anxious to close the cavern of years spent apart. Alex, aware that her hands were trembling, thrust them into her jacket pockets. They were too old to be awkward, certainly too sophisticated to stammer. Her mind shouted, *Calm down, stop overreacting!*

As always, Ted seemed to know what she needed to hear. "You're the same lovely Alex. You've still got that style and those eyes that sparkle."

His reassurance helped her relax; she searched to return his compliments but hesitated instead. The Florida sun had baked the softness from his skin, leaving ridges behind and only a trace of a once-smooth face. The middle button on his coat strained to conceal a formerly svelte waistline, and his once-firm chin had relented into an expanded collar. Ted had aged, perhaps not gracefully, but inevitably. To Alex none of this mattered. His smile was all she saw. So she told him. He looked at her as no one else had ever looked at her, and his eyes smiled, too.

"My God, it looks like we're sequestered in the French embassy!" Ted observed the room's elaborate furnishings, focusing especially on the big, bountiful bed.

"Did you sleep well last night, hon? You always did like a softer mattress."

Alex smiled at his playfulness and replied, "Well, I thought it was fine, but why don't you get comfortable and see for yourself?"

"Good idea, I'll check it out. I've been in this suit since early morning."

A nearby chair suddenly became a convenient recipient of his day's apparel.

"Come join me, beautiful," he said, patting the pillow beside him.

With an invitation she couldn't refuse, Alex slid in next to him.

Ted immediately grasped her hand as if to assure himself that she was real, that this was actually happening. The years spent apart floated into obscurity as they reached for each other, reigniting the torrent they'd once known. His hands moved swiftly, discarding encumbering clothing so that they were free to feel the warmth of each other's nakedness.

"Why did I ever let you go, my lovely Alex? I've missed you, the softness of your skin, the sweet scent of your hair against my chest."

Immersed in pleasure, Alex could not reply. The world outside forgotten, they had recaptured a passion others only dream of.

Fulfilling as it was, they could not feast on love alone. Eventually Ted sat up in bed, claiming that he was ravenous. With humor he announced romance had given him an appetite, so he called room service to order a splendid dinner for two, including an extravagant bottle of wine with which to toast themselves.

Outside, snowflakes whipped against the windows, warning of impending intrusion. Ted, with Alex's encouragement, pretended it was too risky to leave. He'd never catch a cab in such weather but might catch a cold standing in the elements. They teasingly agreed he must stay the night. Within minutes Ted feigned a yawn, insisting it had been a long, tiring day. He was again ready for bed. Alex took a satin gown from her suitcase. It had cost a small fortune for a minimum of fabric designed to be worth every cent. When she came back into the room Ted was already in bed. He looked surprised.

"Why so modest? You used to have me undress you in the hallway!"

"Self-conscious, I guess. Gravity, darling. Besides, this was such an extravagance that I wanted to at least put it on."

She lay down beside him. The gown reached the floor less than one minute after the coverlet. "Ten bucks a second," Ted quipped. They couldn't help but laugh.

"You're beautiful, Alexandra. Just as I left you."

"Oh, Ted, I'm too chubby and ..."

"Be quiet."

The TV played soft music. Somewhere an orchestra had recorded lush melodies so that lovers everywhere could be swept away to their own private ballroom, dancing to the rhythm they alone could hear.

Younger once again, each clung to the memory of what they had felt for each other, the tenderness that had withstood the anguish of separation. When finally he slept, she lay in his arms, tucked near his heart. Content in her momentary fantasy of living out her life in his embrace.

A knock on the door abruptly awakened them. It was the maid, who apologized, saying she'd come back later. Ted bolted straight up.

"Damn, we forgot the Do Not Disturb sign. What time is it anyhow?" His watch on the nightstand indicated late morning. Alex was already running the shower and attempting to repair her usual tousled morning appearance.

"Hon, let's go get something to eat." He pulled back the draperies to see that last night's precipitation had relented. "Looks like a café right across the street—right there near the corner." Alex shouted over the rainfall of water that she'd be out in a minute. It was Ted's turn, and before she could finish dressing he was ready and waiting for her.

"What takes a woman so long?" he joked, not stopping to hear the answer.

Alex held his arm tightly as they maneuvered across the slushy street, glad to reach the comfort of the coffee shop. The aroma of freshly brewed mocha wafted across the small room, beckoning two hungry customers and tempting them to order the special buttermilk pancakes with warm blueberry syrup. Ted ate like an athlete after an event. Alex smiled to herself. The night before had certainly been eventful!

The server had poured a second, then third cup of coffee when Ted got the phone message: due to improved conditions, flights to Florida were now rescheduled for later in the day. "I can catch an earlier plane back to Boca," he exclaimed, sounding pleased.

Alex felt her fingers tighten around the cup's handle. Her hands stiffened, as did her whole body. "Don't be so happy to leave. We're never together. Now you can't wait to go home?"

"I'm sorry, Alex. I didn't mean it that way. It was just an impulse reaction."

"You gave yourself away, Ted. You reacted with your gut. Good old Alex, my convenient bed partner. I can have my fun and go back to my wife!"

"Alex, don't talk like that. You're being ridiculous."

"I'm ridiculous? I'm honest! You're the one who's being impossible."

"For God's sake, keep your voice down, Alex. Let's get out of here before everyone hears our business."

Ted tore a wad of dollars from his wallet and, slamming them on the table, stormed out the door without waiting for Alex to put on her coat. Walking back to the hotel, struggling with tangled sleeves against the cold, she nearly slipped on an icy curb. Ted stopped, grabbed her, and led her back to their room. The maid had just finished—fortunately for her.

"Alright, let's have this thing out. What the hell is wrong with you? All I said was I could get a plane out tonight. You knew I'd be going home—to my family—so why are you so angry? It's always been that way. We've always had an understanding."

"Ted, I'm not angry. I'm hurt. We finally get a chance to be together, and you rush away from me. Who knows if we'll ever have another opportunity like this?"

"Alex, my darling, you've always known I have obligations. I can't give you what you want. I can't give you *me*. Jean and I— we've been together too many years. We've built a history together. I've never explained this to you. Her father was my father's banker. I was barely out of school, a young guy with grandiose ideas of going into business. Jean's family took a chance and loaned me enormous capital. Years later, when my partner swindled me and I filed Chapter 11, my father-in-law invested in me again. Sure, I parlayed that money and became successful, but I couldn't have done it without the initial help." Ted shook his head, as though by doing so he could shrug off his next thought: "Jean reminds me frequently."

"But Ted, you've repaid her over and over again with a marvelous life. Give her all the stupid money she wants. She can have everything—being a socialite in Boca Raton, the grandchildren nearby. Who knows, she could meet a rich widower." Her anguish was evident as her voice grew in intensity. "Stop making excuses to me! You don't have an obligation to give Jean your life. This 'loyalty' toward her father's money is just a convenient cover-up. All these years I've hung in there with you, hoping someday ... but I guess I was playing a losing game all along."

"Enough, Alex, enough! I've thought this through a thousand times, and it always ends the same: it doesn't work. It would never work. If I did leave, if we were together, we'd jeopardize everything we've ever had. We couldn't survive if we built our happiness on someone else's pain. In time the guilt, the remorse, would erode me, and I'd take it out on you. We'd end up resenting each other. You don't want to believe me, but I know it would happen."

"But what are you giving Jean now? You're both living a charade."

"Alex, my beautiful Alex, be reasonable. Look at the life you've made without me—how amazing you are."

"But every night I get in bed without you."

"Well, you haven't been too lonely. How about that musician in New Orleans? You certainly did more than turn over the sheet music for him." Ted smiled at his own witty implication.

"Not funny, Ted. I only went with him because I wanted the excitement. My life was so mundane—for once I wanted to throw ordinary out the window."

"Did you love him?"

Alex replied slowly. She had given her answer much thought. "Yes, I loved Charlie. But I wasn't *in* love with him. There's quite a difference, you know."

Ted nodded. Alex continued, "Why didn't you stop me, tell me no? All it would have taken was two words: don't go. But you never said them."

"I had no right to stop you. I had nothing to offer you."

"Well, what was I to do, waste my life waiting? Oh, Ted, darling, don't leave. Don't throw away what little time we have left."

Ted's face tightened into a near grimace. His speech was pained and nearly inaudible. "I can't let Jean grow old alone."

"But it's all right for me? You're a fool. Don't you realize what we have together—what most people spend their lives searching for? You're tossing it all away as though it doesn't matter."

"Hold on, Alex, you're greatly mistaken. I'm acutely aware of what we could have had together. I have to live with the regret every day. I've been a disappointment to you—and to myself.

It's shadowed my very existence. And there's nothing I can do to make it better."

Ted took her in his arms, as if by the gesture he could shield her from the hurt he'd just inflicted.

"I've wanted you since the first time I saw you in the culinary school—and I've never wanted—loved you—more than I do today. But I can't, beautiful, I just can't."

"I guess that's it then, Ted. We started as friends, and we're back to the beginning. We'll remain friends, but I can't remember when I wasn't in love with you. What a sad epitaph: three lives, and nobody got what they wanted, the happiness in life they deserved. It's the way it is—the way it has to be."

Alex broke his embrace. She stared blankly into space. A sound too plaintive to be a sigh, but too sad to be a laugh, formed into words that tumbled out. "Perhaps in another life. Damn it all, I always did have lousy timing."

Ted mumbled something about having to grab his luggage at his hotel. He spoke so softly that his apology, if there was one, was indistinguishable. Alex did not watch him leave, preferring to look away. Then she called the airline and rescheduled a ticket home on the next flight available.

There were no tears. She was beyond that. She would go home, where her name was respected in the community for all she'd achieved. She would go home and use the years ahead to her advantage—and to everyone else's benefit. Love would come in other ways.

20

LADY LEISURE

A wakening in her own bed, Alex glanced around the room, disappointed for the moment that embroidered butterflies had flown from the walls and a silken canopy had not shaded the streaming sunlight from her eyes. She had forfeited the luxurious French boudoir to another occupant in exchange for this new morning, when she could awake without being embarrassed about disheveled hair. She was home, with no concern if the cellulite on her thighs caught the early light. Ted was not there to notice.

After quick calls to David and Jason at Lilith, her next priority was Garrett—and an apology for leaving New York without seeing his restaurant. How could she possibly explain the reason for such a sudden departure without telling the truth? Alex told herself she had to unpack. Then she read the mail. By midmorning she was out of excuses. It was nearing the noon hour on the East Coast. Garrett would be preparing lunch, too rushed to talk long. A perfect time. Alex phoned, still apprehensive about what to say.

"Garrett, dear, it's me, Alex. I know you're busy, so I'll be quick—I want to apologize for not stopping by the restaurant to say goodbye. With the bad weather my flight was changed, so I left for home unexpectedly."

"Oh, Ms. S., I understand, but I am disappointed. I wanted to treat you to lunch here. Hopefully next time."

Alex joked back, "It's nice to know there's still such a thing as a free lunch." They laughed as old friends comfortably do.

"Ms. S., it's great talking to you, but I'm staring at a dozen orders in front of me. Thanks for calling. It was wonderful seeing you."

Alex put down the phone and felt a huge sense of relief. *There, that's over, as gracefully as possible. Now to get on with my day.*

Suzanne was anxious to hear every detail of the book event. With grand gestures Alex reenacted the manager's impression, including her jeweled eyewear strut. She spoke of being confined in the Cozy Nook and besieged with inquiries from the food columnists—questioning which, if any, of the interviews would appear in print.

Alex shifted uneasily in her chair, assuming she had divulged enough. But Suzanne probed relentlessly. "I'm picking up something else, Alex. Nothing you've said. It's just there in your manner; the way you've been holding yourself so tightly. What went wrong?"

Alex could not answer. Suzanne was her boss, her associate in business. Much as she wanted to shut the office door and shout and thrash and scream into space, "How dare you hurt me when I've done nothing but love you?" she could not speak of what Suzanne suspected. Perhaps someday, when the wound had healed. But not today.

Alex stood up and smoothed her skirt, successfully avoiding Suzanne's eyes. The moment was over, fractured by the unspoken plea: *Please don't invade my privacy.*

Suzanne, intuitive as she was, sensed the request and quickly changed the subject. "There's a new restaurant opening near the stadium. I suppose it'll be burgers and beer, but it might be fun for you to try."

Alex, grateful for the reprieve, agreed, and the two women said their goodbyes.

Despite what else goes on in life, the sun manages to break through each morning. Alex settled into her everyday routine, becoming more comfortable as time raced ahead.

John, her editor, eventually retired. Actually, he was forced to by some heart problems attributed to his lifestyle of doing everything wrong. As a result, the format changed. Alex was promoted to assistant food editor. It was an easier job, allowing her to work out recipes at home much of the time. Driving at night—especially in winter—had become difficult. Eating odd and sometimes poorly prepared food upset her stomach. It was time for a younger critic to pick up the fork.

In a way, working from her own kitchen brought Alex back to the beginning, experimenting with classic recipes, developing new flavor combinations. She reminisced about those long-forgotten days when she and her friend Mary had invented the *Alexandra the Grate* cuisine.

Every once in a while, as though he could detect when her hands were crusted in crumbs, Ted would call. Just like that. Always kind and gentle, he'd ask what she was doing, patiently listening to details about the food prepared for the next edition. Taking the cue when it was his turn to talk, he'd speak of his children—marveling that his grandson had grown so tall, nearly his own height. There was never a mention of another rendezvous. The conversation usually closed with his latest medical diagnosis—a stiff back, a sore knee—and how he didn't like this aging business. Alex would listen, trying to soothe where it hurt. Then she'd put down the phone and smile. She was still his best friend.

For the first time in many years, money was not a problem. Thanks to David's financial prowess, the amount he'd invested for her increased and a welcomed check arrived at the start of each month.

David and Julie were building a fine life together, immersed in their careers. Content to be together without a marriage certificate, they were not interested in having a family. Although she never said as much to them, Alex regretted not having a grandchild. She often saw magazine ads showing grandmas baking sugar cookies with delighted children looking on. She clung to the sweet image, hoping that someday she, too, would qualify.

The trees outside her kitchen window altered with each season from a wondrous palette of forest green to garnet crisp to barren. Then from nowhere spring would arrive, bursting with pink and ivory blossoms. Alex counted the colors, each one representing time slipping from her grasp. She tried hard, holding tight to each day, but like the one before, it escaped from her touch and melded into the midnight air.

There came a time when Alex finally felt close enough to confide in Suzanne about that episode in New York. Maybe their friendship had deepened, or maybe it was a need for closure. But it happened spontaneously over, of all things, a tuna sandwich. A special food section had been planned for Easter, complete with photos of festive brunches. Suzanne came to the shoot, along with Annie, the page editor, and Alex. It took longer than expected—far past lunchtime—to complete the extensive layout. Annie, late for an appointment, rushed back to the office. But Suzanne suggested that she and Alex grab a quick something at a neighboring restaurant.

They ate and chattered about the morning's work. Then, without any logic, Alex felt an overwhelming need to relinquish a burden she'd struggled with for far too long before finally chiseling it into fragments to be tossed away. When Alex had exhausted both her rhetoric and herself, Suzanne wisely did not criticize or condone. Instead, searching for some humor, she said what a friend could say.

"You certainly have unusual taste in men! You've mentioned your former husband, Steven, and I've heard comments about Charlie—and now this fellow."

"Yes, three times and out!"

"They could be characters in your next book."

"Not a chance!"

Suzanne's voice lowered, and her words came slowly. "To experience love is beautiful. Never regret it, because it's touched you so deeply. All that has happened—even the sadness—has made you into the extraordinary person you are. Know that, and be kind to yourself."

Alex could only manage a nod in response. Suzanne glanced at her watch, exclaiming that the afternoon was half over and she should get back to work. She motioned to the server and paid the bill, and the two women got up from the table, leaving their intimate conversation behind. They would never speak of the experience again.

21

BRAVO!

Birthdays celebrated and years marked upward, in contrast with the height of Alex's heels, which diminished down to sensible. Ted continued to call when he thought of it—usually after his cholesterol report. Thanks to Suzanne's intervention, Alex drew a paycheck even though her assignments lightened. She realized this arrangement could not go on much longer when her friend spoke frequently about retiring to Arizona. She'd had quite enough of the Midwestern winters.

For the first time since she could remember, Alex did not live by the clock. If she felt lazy, the bed went unmade; if there was a foreign film playing, she could see a movie in the afternoon—and pour butter on the popcorn. To add to her comfort, the soufflé book was still selling—slowly but steadily—on Amazon. Life felt secure. She had paid her dues to enjoy each day.

When Garrett called, asking a favor, Alex was jarred from complacency.

"Ms. S. I have another cookbook in the works, *Restaurant*

Recipes for the Home Cook. I'd really like you to write the introduction. You know, accolades, a sales pitch."

"Oh, Garrett, I'm so flattered. Of course I'll do it for you. It's
an honor!"

"Thanks, Ms. S.! I'll send you the details and—"

"May I read the manuscript? It would help me to grasp the
right character—the essence."

Garrett laughed. "Of course. I was so excited to ask you, I
forgot about the contents. I'll have the publisher send you a
paper copy as soon as possible. Thanks, Ms. S., I knew I could
count—"

Alex interrupted, "You always can, Garrett, my friend.
Always know I'm here for you."

Alex smiled the rest of the day, pleased to have been
thought of with such respect. She immediately began playing
with ideas. A well-written intro was imperative.

Several weeks later a large package arrived, so securely
bundled that Alex had to argue with the scissors to release its
contents. Inside the bubble wrap was a pile of papers: Garrett's
newest and possibly best book-to-be. Alex grabbed it out of its
manila casings, anxious to spend the necessary hours studying
each page. As she scrutinized every recipe for accuracy, her prodigy
was again in her classroom under her discriminating glare. Every
ingredient and technique was analyzed. Of course Alex realized it
was not her job to be critical, but habit compelled her to do so.

Most of the manuscript was accurate, but she did make a
few suggestions, hoping they would be received well. When she
had finished the text, Alex started composing the copy. Not too
effusive with adjectives. It had to be believable, a synopsis that
readers could relate to, convincing them to buy this book
instead of the others available.

It wasn't an easy task. Alex wrote and then rewrote three,
even four times. When a paragraph seemed okay she'd walk

away for a time, returning to read it again to get the impact of her words. Was it clear? Did it say all it could?

Alex composed it as she did the laundry, as she lay restless in bed waiting for sleep—even driving to the dentist's office. It had to stop; she was creating her own problem.

"I'm trying too hard. If I just calm down it will come together," she told herself. With that in mind, she sat down at the computer and let the words flow as smoothly as Garrett's hollandaise sauce. Starting with a reference to Garrett's Garage, she followed with his many accomplishments intertwined with personal qualities. Threading it all together, she concluded with a recommendation that the book belonged in everyone's library or kitchen. She read it over, slept on it that night, and in the morning sent it without hesitation to Garrett and his editor with a cover letter stating she would certainly make any changes if necessary. Then Alex made herself a cup of herbal tea, ate two chocolate chip cookies, and waited quite impatiently for a response.

It was a short wait. The editor sent a brief thank-you, noting that, with the exception of a few comments, the copy was most acceptable. He even used the word *interesting*.

"Ms. S., it's me. Sorry it's late, but I had to call. I'm really impressed with your writing. I can tell it's from the heart and you meant every word. It's great, thank you."

"I tried to catch the personality of your book and you as well. I hope it helps. I know the introduction makes the initial impression."

"You'll get the first copy when it's published."

"Garrett, dear, I'd like to talk longer—" A huge yawn interrupted her.

"Oh, I'm sorry. I didn't realize it was that late," he said.

"Well, it really isn't. It's just that I get sleepy earlier now. My eyes automatically shut by ten. It comes with age, you know.

But enough about me. Let's talk about your book. I'm so pleased I could help you."

"That's why I called. I wanted to tell you you're wonderful. I don't know how my life would have turned out without everything you've given me. You've shown me how to keep going no matter what happens."

"Oh, Garrett, you don't need to butter me up!" Alex quipped. "From one chef to another."

But Garrett wouldn't let her brush him off with humor. "Look at all you've done—all the people you've inspired—and what you've accomplished."

"Stop exaggerating, now. I've never discovered a medical cure or built a skyscraper. All I did was cook and—"

Garrett interrupted, "You've made people smile and feel happy, and that in itself is a gift."

"Oh, my friend, you are too generous. I just hope my world knows I've been in it. And perhaps it's a bit better for my effort."

There was a pause before Garrett spoke again, this time softly, more intensely. "Trust me, we know that. So many of us know. And we are grateful to you, Alex."

"Garrett, you finally called me by my first name!"

"It's time. It's the right time. Well, I've got to let you go, but before I say good night, I needed to tell you that you've always been spectacular."

"Oh, Garrett, I appreciate your kindness, but please don't describe me in past tense. I may be older—I may never again dance on the moon—but whatever tomorrow brings, whatever life throws in my way, I'm willing to take a deep breath and put one foot in front of the other. I don't know where I'm headed, but I'm damn sure I'm not through yet!"

Alex imagined Garrett's smile, his nod of approval as he wished her sweet dreams.

And the phone clicked off.

ALSO BY MARGIE ZATS

Great Recipes from Someone Who Loves to Eat

Stories from Someone Older than Television

A Platter of Chatter: Charming Stories and Terrific Recipes

Alexandra the Grate, Who Insisted Life be Well Done

CPSIA information can be obtained
at www.ICGtesting.com
Printed in the USA
FFHW020022070919
54839665-60522FF

9 781634 899475